COURAGE IN THE MOUNTAIN WILDERNESS

CALL OF THE ROCKIES ~ BOOK 4

MISTY M. BELLER

Copyright © 2021 Misty M. Beller

All rights reserved. No portion of this book may be reproduced or transmitted in any form or by any means - photocopied, shared electronically, scanned, stored in a retrieval system, or other - without the express permission of the publisher. Exceptions will be made for brief quotations used in critical reviews or articles promoting this work.

The characters and events in this fictional work are the product of the author's imagination. Any resemblance to actual people, living or dead, is coincidental.

Unless otherwise indicated, all Scripture quotations are taken from the Holy Bible, Kings James Version.

ISBN: 978-1-942265-38-2

It is of the Lord's mercies that we are not consumed, because his compassions fail not.
They are new every morning: great is thy faithfulness.
The Lord is my portion, saith my soul; therefore will I hope in him.

Lamentations 3:22-24 (KJV)

CHAPTER 1

Early Spring, 1831
Clearwater River Valley, Future Idaho Territory

*E*ven as a grown man, Caleb Jackson still craved the familiar.

And the sight of the familiar Nez Perce camp stretching out ahead of him settled around Caleb like the soft blanket he'd carried far too long through his boyhood years.

It'd been weeks since he and his friends had left this village, and they'd been to two other camps since. But something about this one had seeped into his soul and felt a little more like home. A strange feeling when he didn't even speak their tongue.

Maybe he'd connected with this place because the people here had been so welcoming. His first taste of the Nimiipuu way of life.

It didn't hurt that the maidens were quite pleasant to look at. Especially one in particular, although perhaps she wouldn't be called a maiden. She'd been married once, and from what he'd gathered, her husband had died just before the birth of their son. A cute little chap about two years old with chubby legs who seemed to get into trouble an awful lot.

Movement to the right of the camp near the river swung his gaze that way. Surely that couldn't be the lad he'd just been thinking of, toddling away from the lodges toward the deep currents.

The figure was definitely a child around the age of River Boy.

Caleb's heart hurtled into his throat, and he spun his horse toward the lad, digging in his heels. The mare sprang into action, surging to a canter. He pushed her faster as he bent low over her neck.

Hadn't the lad learned his lesson the last time he played too close to the water's edge? Joel and Adam had barely saved him from freezing to death when his leg had caught in the ice crusting the murky surface. Joel had narrowly escaped with his own life when the ice broke through while they crossed back over the river to safety.

Caleb squeezed his legs tighter, urging the mare faster to close the last thirty strides. The boy had only two steps to reach the bank now. Where was his mother? How could he have wandered all the way out of town? Again.

With no father to provide for the family, she must be carrying the burden of too much responsibility on her shoulders to keep such an active child contained. A situation he was far too familiar with.

Determination surged through him as the lad splashed into the water, his black head dipping with each step he toddled down the bank.

Caleb locked his eyes on those dark locks and pushed the mare harder. The puff of hair dropped lower when the boy sat quickly. Maybe his feet had been jerked from under him by the swift-flowing current. At least there was no ice now. Was that a good thing? The snow melt from the mountains had filled the river, rising up to burst over its banks.

The mare neared, and Caleb sat back in the saddle, pulling hard on the reins to slow his horse. He leapt to the ground before she stopped and sprinted the last strides to the bank even as the boy's dark hair floated away from the bank.

A child's laugh sounded, and the boy splashed in the rushing water, despite the fact that it was carrying him far from shore—faster and faster with each heartbeat. Did he not know the swift current held his life in its clutch? The lad knew no fear. Especially not the healthy kind.

Caleb raced three long strides along the bank's edge, just far enough to get ahead of where the boy floated. Then he launched into the icy liquid. The cold sucked his breath, clamping hard on his chest with its frigid claws.

Gathering his wits, he mentally scrambled for anything he could recall about how quickly the water deepened. The stretch nearest the bank dipped to waist level. But with the extra snow melt flowing down from the mountains, Caleb had to break into a swim after only one step. Three hard strokes brought him within reach of the lad.

He grabbed an arm and held tight, planting his feet in front of him and paddling backward to stop the river's grip.

Drawing the boy close to his chest, Caleb turned and swam toward the shore. A group of people had gathered there—his friends, from the quick glance he managed between swimming strokes.

At last, hands reached out to him, one grabbing his arm and the others taking the boy. Still laughing, River Boy kicked his pudgy arms and legs the whole way up.

For Caleb's part, exhaustion weighed his bone-chilled limbs now that fear no longer drove him. He pulled himself up on the bank, crawling to a dry spot to sit.

"Here, Caleb, let's get you out of these wet things." Susanna,

Beaver Tail's wife, crouched in front of him and began unbuttoning his coat. She was right. The furs had taken on water, and maybe its weight was part of what stole his strength.

He took over unfastening the elkhorn buttons and slipped the heavy coat off. His buckskin tunic underneath was mostly dry, except around the collar, sleeves, and waist.

He glanced up at Susanna with a nod of thanks. "That's better."

Now that he'd caught most of his breath and a little of his energy, he turned to where the boy was being tended to.

His gaze landed on an image that once again stole his breath. The lad's mother ran to her son. While he watched, she cradled him in a tight embrace.

Otskai was even more beautiful than Caleb's memories of her. Her face clear. Not a wrinkle or blemish to be found. So young. His heart ached. She was too young to already be a widow, raising this boy on her own.

Then she lifted her dark lashes and cast her wide gaze toward Caleb. The whites of her eyes glimmered red, so full of unshed tears that the pressure in his chest tightened tenfold.

"Thank you." Her words came out in a thick accent, but she spoke English. The first he'd heard from her.

The weight on his chest loosened enough for his heart to ramp into another gallop. What was wrong with him, letting himself fall so hard for a woman he barely knew?

He felt for her predicament, the way she must have worried over her son and the boy's penchant for danger. But Caleb had never thought to feel anything more than concern for her.

He forced his gaze away from hers, letting his focus drop to the toddler. The lad curled against her, cheek resting on her shoulder with a thumb in his mouth. Perfectly content in the loving protection of her arms.

A burn crept up Caleb's throat. They made such a perfect picture, this woman and boy. He barely knew them, but the pair had already managed to plant themselves firmly in his thoughts, even when he was an entire mountain range away.

He needed some space. With a flick of his gaze to her eyes, he nodded. "You're welcome." He wanted to know how the boy had wandered away by himself, again, but he'd have to ask that later.

For now, he grabbed his coat and pushed to standing, then marched toward his mare. He owed the girl a walk to dry her sweaty sides and a good brushing. Maybe that would give them both enough time to cool off.

OTSKAI CLUTCHED her son to her chest as she watched the big man gather his horse's reins and lead her away. She should stand and take River Boy back to their lodge, but fear had leaked away all her strength. How many times would this boy scare her lifeless?

So far, these white men had saved River Boy twice. Both times, her son would have died if they hadn't reached him in time. Neither time had she been there. She'd not been what her child needed. The guilt would smother her if she let it, but she couldn't give in to such weakness.

River Boy squirmed in her tight hold, a good reminder that she had to get him back to the lodge and out of his wet clothes. The last thing he needed was a sickness from the remnants of this winter wind.

After pressing a final kiss to his damp hair, she stood and gripped his chubby little hand. The lad tried to dart ahead, but she'd learned to keep a tight hold.

One of the Nimiippu women who'd come with the white men was lingering nearby, and Otskai worked for a smile. "Elan?" She remembered this one, from a village of the Pikunin band to the north. The first time she'd met Elan, she'd been struck by the fact that the meaning of her name matched her personality—friendly.

The woman nodded with a return smile that didn't mask the concern in her eyes. "I see River Boy is still living up to his name."

Otskai sent a wry look toward the rushing water, fighting off the shiver that always coursed through her at the sight of the churning current. "Perhaps if I change his name, he'll change his ways."

Her deceased husband's parents had christened the lad River Boy after his first escapade in the water, back when he could only crawl. He'd been in their care while she worked to scrape a new batch of furs. The lad had crawled right to the edge of the bank and tumbled head-over-toes into the water.

She'd been so relieved they pulled him out safely that she'd accepted the new name. Especially since she'd never really liked the one Motsqueh had given him before his birth. *Kapskaps timine*, Strong-willed One. He'd given the name because River Boy had been so active inside her belly, she'd learned after the boy was born that his movement sprang from too much energy. Not too strong a will.

Maybe if she'd fought this new title, her son wouldn't have developed this deadly love of rushing water. It seemed no matter how careful she was, he still found a way to sneak out of her focus and escape to the river.

She forced back those thoughts and turned toward the camp, tightening her grip on her son's hand. "I must get him back and changed."

Elan fell into step on River Boy's other side. "Can I walk with you? Joel has my horse, and I need to find my aunt and uncle to see if we can use their extra lodge while we're here."

Otskai didn't answer the question. She would have preferred to be alone, but she liked this woman. "You're staying long this time?"

Elan shook her head. "My husband's brother has business with your chief. Once that is finished, we'll return to the village of my people." She sent Otskai a grin. "I think. My husband and his brother seem drawn to adventure, so I don't know how firmly we'll stick to that plan. We left my dog there with my parents, so I hope we're not gone from him too long."

Husband. The last time they'd been here, Otskai well remembered Elan pining over one of the two white men who had been ill. The two who had saved River Boy. And yes, she also remembered the little dog. The one who'd been injured by a pack of wolves outside of camp. That was probably why they left the animal behind this time. It may even be still recovering.

She raised her brows. "You're married now?"

A pretty flush spread across her face, a sign this was a very new event. And it surely was, for it had been less than two moons since they'd left, if she remembered correctly.

Elan dipped her chin in a nod. "To Joel. He's the one who'd been shot before." Elan pressed a hand to her belly to show the place the bullet had struck. Then all trace of pleasure left her face. She must have remembered the part Joel played in saving River Boy.

Better to speak of that day openly so it wouldn't hang heavily between them. "He's the one who nearly died saving my son." She met the woman's eyes boldly. "I owe a huge debt to him. And to the other man for his bravery this day. You're all welcome to anything I have. Including space in my lodge."

She hadn't thought ahead to that offer, but it seemed the only decent thing to say. The tiny teepee she and her son shared was barely big enough to hold their supplies, but they could move outside to sleep if they needed to. She couldn't withhold shelter from these people who had done what she'd been unable to. Twice now.

Elan's smile was soft. "You owe us nothing, but I thank you for the offer. My aunt's lodge is large and should be more than we need. We would love for you to share a meal with us though. Perhaps tomorrow at sunset?" Elan's gaze probed, seeking out agreement.

Otskai nodded. In truth, she couldn't deny them such a simple request. Yet something inside her said more time spent with these newcomers might disrupt all the hard work she'd put into building her future.

Yet how could it? This was simply a meal, one more opportunity to express gratitude for another selfless act.

Good thing she'd been learning to speak the white man's tongue.

CHAPTER 2

This fence had to last until River Boy was old enough to know better than to sneak off alone to the river. Hopefully, by then he would be able to swim.

Caleb hoisted the narrow tree trunk up to stack on top of the others. This last one should make the fence tall enough. He gripped the spot where the ends met the next fence section to form an X. He'd flattened the places where the ends of the logs stacked to make them lie better, and that would hold for a few days. He should cut some nails to drive through the wood, though.

He settled his hatchet in the strap at his waist, then reached down to scoop up the strips of bark that had peeled off while he was working. He sent a final scan around the place. Each lodge had only a small yard, so it hadn't taken long to cut enough wood to fence the little section in front of Otskai's door flap.

Working out how to manage a gate had been the most challenging part. Hopefully, she wouldn't mind lifting a log or two when she needed to pass through.

He tried to see the spot from her perspective. Her legs were much shorter than his. Actually, every part of her. Would she think this solution to keep her boy contained was silly? He scanned the other lodges around hers. None had anything even close to this. This fence singled out her home from the others. Would it make her feel different?

This new worry needled through him like a worm eating an apple. He'd never been good at foreseeing a woman's opinion about anything, especially a woman he barely knew.

She might hate this.

So...he'd let her look at it, then offer to take the logs down if she didn't like it.

Voices sounded behind him, the low murmur of a woman, then the high giggle of a child.

A glance over his shoulder sent his heart racing again. He worked for a smile as he turned to face her.

Otskai held her son high as he sat on her arm. The position made Caleb think she'd been tickling him, maybe to keep him from squirming out of her arms.

But now they both turned their focus to him. Otskai's gaze was curious, and the moment it slipped past him to the lodge and the new fence, her eyes widened.

He didn't breathe as he waited for signs of anger. But her brows didn't draw together, her mouth didn't pinch in a frown. Her jaw dropped open, in fact.

When River Boy wiggled, she lowered him to the ground. The boy scampered forward and went straight for a rail. Caleb had judged the height well, for the fence rose a good head above the lad's. The boy peered through the gap between two logs.

Caleb strode toward him and reached under his arms. "You want to go inside?" He hoisted the lad and lifted him over the rail, then set him down in the yard.

Now he had to face the woman and explain why he thought it would be a good idea to alter her home without her consent.

He turned to her, his apology ready, and found her studying the fence. "I thought this might help keep the lad contained, but it's as easy to take down as it was to put up. Even easier, and I can chop the logs into firewood for you."

She stepped nearer and paused at the gate. She didn't say a word, or even look at Caleb. Her gaze simply roamed the fence from one side to the other, surely taking in how her son was running in circles, staying easily within the confines.

Caleb stepped closer to her, near enough to work the gate. "To walk through, I made bars for these outside rails to fit in. Just lift the rails off, but you might only want to remove the top rail most of the time."

He pulled the log away, then started to reach for the second one. But before he could grab it, she stepped over it.

For several heartbeats, he stood there holding the piece, watching her. Should he follow her in or replace the log and stay on the outside?

He didn't want to stay on the outside, neither outside her fence nor outside her life.

And that fact sent a sobering wash of reality through him. There was a line between caring for widows and orphans as the Bible instructed and letting his heart become involved. Better he stay put right here than tiptoe across that dividing mark.

So he remained outside the fence. But he didn't replace the rail.

Otskai examined his work on both sides, including where he'd driven stakes at the edges of her lodge to secure the log ends as close to the stretched hide as possible.

Finally, she turned to him and approached, a smile playing at the corners of her mouth. A beautiful sight.

Her chin dipped a little in shyness as she neared him. Maybe he should offer again to take the fence down. But before he could, she spoke those same words she'd said after he'd pulled her son from the river.

"Thank you." Then she seemed to work for her next words. "Is good."

He couldn't stop the grin that stretched all the way across his face. As hard as she'd worked for that last bit, she probably hadn't understood much of his nervous rambling from before.

He tried for easy words and spoke slower this time. "If you don't want the fence, we can cut it for firewood." He pointed toward the logs, then made the motion of chopping them and throwing the pieces into a fire.

She shook her head firmly, leaving no doubt of her opinion. "Is good."

Caleb breathed out a long puff of air to loosen the tension in his chest. "Well." He glanced toward the boy who was attempting somersaults in the low grass. Even when each roll ended sideways, the lad wasn't deterred. He was cute as a half grown pup and twice as determined. Caleb chuckled.

Then he turned his focus back to the woman. "I'll leave you be then." And with a two-finger wave, he turned from her piercing eyes and headed back to his lodge.

Now maybe he could cease thinking about these two and focus on what he'd really come here to do—help Adam retrieve the lost treasure he'd sworn to recover before he would marry Meksem.

"I JUST DON'T KNOW what I have that's worth anything."

Caleb studied Adam as his words weighed heavy in the air. The man turned away to watch their small herd of horses grazing, the pensive look on his face speaking of more than just his worries. Adam still possessed a thread of insecurity, although Caleb knew well that God was replacing that feeling, little by little.

Adam turned to look at Caleb and Joel, who stood on Caleb's other side. "I'm grateful that Meksem loved me enough to trade her most prized possession for Tesoro." His gaze flicked to the striking spotted Palouse gelding Adam's soon-to-be-bride had given him.

His brow tightened even more. "But I can't let her lose that tomahawk. It was the only thing she had left from her father. The tool is special enough without the family value, what with the gem inlaid in the handle. When I speak with the chief, I need to have something to offer in trade to get it back. But I have nothing. Only the horse she traded in the first place, but I promised Meksem I wouldn't give him up."

Caleb studied the man as his mind worked through everything Adam possessed. Not much by way of earthly goods. Only two horses, one being the fine spotted gelding, the other a plain bay that wouldn't be worth much in the eyes of the Nez Perce chief already rich in quality horse flesh.

Other than the animals, he had a saddle, gun, knife, clothing, probably a journal, and maybe a pen and ink. All of it put together still wouldn't be an equal trade for the tomahawk, and Adam would have nothing left.

An idea slipped in as his gaze drifted down Adam's arms to his expressive hands. Adam's lean muscle was nothing compared to Caleb's own big-boned brawn, but Adam possessed a quickness and wit superior to most. "Maybe instead of giving a possession, you could *do* something for him."

Adam and Joel both turned to Caleb, their gazes scrutinizing. Though the brothers weren't twins, their relation was impossible to miss in their dark, refined features. The orange shade of Adam's eyes could be especially daunting when he probed with their full force.

Like now. "What do you mean?"

Caleb shrugged. "Hunt maybe. Perhaps you could offer to bring in a half dozen elk to feed him and his people through the winter. You could start by offering that and see where the conversation goes."

Adam turned his gaze back to the horses, but the words he

mumbled showed he was deep in thought. "A quest of sorts. Elk might be hard to find after a long winter, but that would make their value even greater. If I could discover even a small herd, the gift might be enough."

Adam settled into silence, and Caleb held his tongue too. That idea had to be the Lord's leading, for the thought certainly wasn't anything Caleb had been mulling over.

At last, Adam nodded, then turned to them with determination marking his features. "A good plan. I'll go speak with the chief now."

Caleb grinned. Adam never let grass grow under his feet when his mind was set.

"Better take Elan with you." Joel's words halted his brother's exuberance.

Adam glanced toward him, brows raised in question.

"To translate. Unless your Nimiiputimpt is better than mine already." Joel tipped a half smile at his brother. Since they would both have Nez Perce wives, or Nimiipuu, as The People called themselves, they were working hard to learn the language. And since they came from Spain and already knew Spanish, French, and English, it made sense both men could easily pick up another language. But the going seemed slow.

Adam nodded. "Good idea." With a slight shift in direction, he slipped back into his determined stride.

Give him favor, Lord. He's gonna need it. Every part of this journey West had turned out to be more adventure—and danger—than Caleb could have ever dreamed. Yet he wouldn't trade even one of the experiences.

But bartering with an Indian chief was one undertaking he'd gladly allow Adam to pursue on his own. Speaking with strangers had never been Caleb's strength, which was one of the many reasons why he'd come on this journey to begin with. He'd simply not been good enough to stand behind the pulpit.

WHAT HAD she been thinking to agree to a meal with the white people?

Otskai pulled another camas root from her underground oven and laid it on the flat rock she would use to carry the hot food to their lodge.

Of course, these new friends weren't all white, so perhaps she should stop calling them that, even in her mind. Two of the women were part of her own tribe, though from a different band. And one of the men was Blackfoot, although if she let herself dwell too much on that fact, she might lose her nerve completely. Blackfoot were rarely kind to her people, although this one didn't seem bent toward malice.

She stood and lifted the flat stone bearing the camas roots. They'd been baking for three sleeps, so each should be perfectly sweetened.

"Come." She reached for River Boy's hand as she spoke the white man's word. She was trying to teach her son everything she was learning in bits and pieces from what little her people knew about the white man's tongue.

He looked at her but didn't come toward her, so she moved forward and grabbed his hand.

As they stepped outside their lodge, a glance at the fence bolstered her courage. She had much to thank these people for. The least she could do was accept their offer to share a meal.

By the time she reached the edge of the campfire they'd built outside their temporary lodge, the rock in her left hand had grown impossibly heavy. She didn't dare release her son, though. He'd become far too independent since he started walking.

As she made out the identity of each person sitting around the fire, one figure stood and moved around the group toward her. Those broad shoulders and his superior height were impossible to miss.

Caleb.

He approached them with a jaunt in his step and spoke a word in his tongue she didn't know.

River Boy wriggled in her hold, but she had to work too much to keep from dropping the food to focus on what the boy wanted. When Caleb bent low to face her son, she realized the boy was reaching for him.

Caleb held out his hands to the lad, then glanced up at her, brows raised as if he was asking permission.

Relief slipped through her. Of course she didn't mind. Perhaps she shouldn't be surprised her fearless son took to these unusual strangers so easily.

As the tall man scooped up River Boy in one arm and rose to his full height, her son giggled. The man grinned at him with a look that no mother could sustain against. How could one not feel drawn to a person who treated her babe with such tender enjoyment?

Then Caleb turned those gentle eyes toward her. His gaze dropped to what she carried, and in a single heartbeat, he stepped forward and scooped the stone platter from her hold with his free hand. His fingers brushed hers in the trade-off. But he stepped back so quickly, she might have imagined the contact if his warmth hadn't seared her skin.

Now that he'd taken both her burdens, he nodded toward the fire. "Come join us." Those words she understood.

Caleb settled her beside Elan in the place where he'd been sitting before. Then he lowered her son beside her and settled himself on the other side of the lad.

Elan greeted her and River Boy in their familiar tongue, and her white husband leaned forward to echo the same halting words. He offered an apologetic grin as he spoke. The accent wasn't perfect, but at least he was trying.

Meksem, the other woman from the Pikunin band, merely raised a hand. The fact that she sat across the fire probably accounted for her quietness. The last time this group had been here, she'd kept herself somewhat apart, although the few times Otskai had spoken with her, it seemed like the woman was simply quiet by nature. Not prideful or conceited. Her training as a warrior probably taught her the value of silence.

The white woman in the group, the one with hair the color of dark honey, spoke something that included the word *food*. Adam's name was also among the sounds she spoke, and another glance around the circle showed that man wasn't present.

Elan turned to her with an apologetic smile as she translated. "My husband's brother has gone to speak with your chief but should join us anytime now. The food is ready to eat when he comes."

Otskai sat straighter. What business did the white man have with her uncle? Maybe they had goods to trade or questions only the chief could answer.

Usually, the white trappers who came asked to speak with the chief first. But this group hadn't been so official the first time they visited. Then they'd left in a hurry when they received news that Meksem's sister had been kidnapped.

Which reminded her, she should inquire about the girl's recovery. She turned her focus to the woman across the campfire. "Did you find success in your journey? Is your sister safe?"

Meksem's face softened in a faint smile as she nodded. "She is."

As the group told the story of the journey to recover Telipe, Otskai wanted to wrap her coat tighter around her. Crossing the mountains during the coldest months was no small feat. This group had done that twice as they rushed to intercept the Blackfoot war party that had kidnapped the Salish women. At least they'd found success and brought all back safely.

"Even Telipe's unborn babe seems unharmed." Meksem's quiet relief sounded through her words.

Otskai eased out a breath. "I'm so glad to hear it."

A motion at the edge of the firelight caught everyone's notice, and the man, Adam, stepped into view. She studied his face as he settled between Meksem and Joel. His lowered brow made his concern clear. If he'd received the same training in masking his emotions that so many of the braves did, he'd not learned the art well. His every thought seemed to cast itself across his features.

"Well?" Joel prompted, giving voice to the expectant silence that had settled over them all.

Adam's gaze slipped around the group, hovering on her for an extra heartbeat.

She wanted to shrink back. She shouldn't be here. This group had a private matter to discuss. She pushed up to standing and reached for River Boy's hand. "We'll go and allow you to speak openly." She didn't know the white man's words, so she used her own. Elan could translate for the others.

But Caleb grabbed her arm. "Wait."

She made the mistake of glancing at his face, and the disappointment marking his features stabbed her chest.

"Stay." This from Adam, and she forced her gaze to him to determine whether he meant the command.

He shook his head. "Don't go." The corners of his mouth turned up in a look she couldn't quite decipher. Almost embarrassment. But not quite.

Then he spoke a string of words she couldn't understand, and she looked to Elan for interpretation.

"He says the news he has involves you." Elan's brow lined in confusion.

A tingle of apprehension slid down Otskai's back, and she eased down to sit again. Something told her she needed very much to hear what this man was about to say.

CHAPTER 3

Caleb kept his body relaxed and his eyes pointed toward Adam as they waited around the campfire for the man to speak of his conversation with the chief. But much of Caleb's focus honed on the woman at the edge of his vision.

Even now, Otskai looked as if she might spring up and dart away. At least the lad was focused on the food Susanna had handed over for him. The boy seemed a healthy weight for a lad his young age, but he ate now as though this was the first time today.

Adam's voice tugged Caleb's focus to his words. "I offered to work off the trade for the tomahawk and mentioned hunting or doing anything else he needed. At first, he looked like he would refuse. Then he thought for a while and finally said there was one thing. If I could bring back this one thing the Shoshone took from him, he'd gladly hand over the tomahawk."

Caleb's pulse leapt. The Shoshone weren't always on friendly terms with the Nez Perce. Surely a few white men would have better chance at getting a stolen item back. Another trek across the mountains might well be the hardest part of the mission, but spring should be coming any day.

"What is it he asked you to bring back for him?" Meksem's quiet question was barely loud enough for everyone to hear. She sounded suspicious, as though she didn't expect it to be as simple as Caleb assumed.

Adam's gaze flicked to Otskai for an instant, then his eyes met Meksem's. "His daughter."

A gasp from the woman nearest him jerked Caleb's gaze to her face. Otskai's mouth pinched tight, her wide eyes studying Adam.

Caleb glanced from her to Adam, who'd turned his focus to Otskai as well. He voiced the first question that sprang to mind. "Was she kidnapped?" Getting her back wouldn't be easy, but they'd already been through this type of mission once. They could return this girl to her father just like they'd recovered Meksem's sister.

But instead of answering, Adam raised his brows as he studied Otskai, as if he wanted her to respond. Maybe the chief hadn't given many details. That would be odd if he really wanted his daughter back.

Caleb looked back at Otskai as Elan spoke a few quiet words in their language.

She gave a single shake of her head in answer. "No. Watkuese left." Her English was clear enough, but the situation still seemed awfully vague.

Caleb floundered for what to ask to get to the root of his questions. "She left...on her own? Ran away? How old is this girl?" He kept his focus on Otskai as Elan translated.

She turned her beautiful face to him, her wide eyes bearing the smallest hint of fear. When she spoke, her voice rose and fell in a melodic rhythm. If only he could understand the words.

Once more, Elan translated. "She says her cousin is a little older than she is. When the Tiiwelka—or the Shoshone, as you call them—came to trade, Watkuese packed her things and left with them."

Otskai spoke again, her focus still on Caleb. He couldn't have looked away from her haunting gaze if he'd wanted to.

Elan interpreted her words again. "Her uncle, the chief, went after them to bring Watkuese back. But she refused to come. She said she wants to make her own way."

While this fascinating woman held his gaze, Caleb was having a bit of trouble focusing on what her words meant and what their band of friends should do about them.

At last, she dropped her gaze to her son to help him with his food. Now, Caleb could muddle through what she'd said.

The most startling fact finally glared up at him. Was Otskai the chief's niece? How had he not known that? He'd only met the man a couple times, and Caleb had been in the background of the conversation because he didn't know the language. Maybe there wasn't a reason he *should've* known that Otskai was a near relation of the man who led this village.

But still…that seemed like an important detail.

"Why does he think Adam can bring her back if she refused to come before?" Joel's question was a good one.

One of the other men in their group, French, leaned forward. "Perhaps he thinks she's realized the error of her ways and would be relieved for someone to come retrieve her." He accompanied his comment with a shrug. "Perhaps."

Elan had begun murmuring to Otskai, probably translating what the others were saying.

Otskai shook her head as Elan finished. Then Otskai responded in English. "Watkuese is…" She paused a second, then spoke a Nimiipuu word to Elan.

Elan smiled as understanding dawned. "Stubborn."

Otskai nodded. "Is stubborn." Her accent hung thick, but the words were clearly discernible in her rolling cadence. "Not come."

Adam leaned forward, resting his elbows on his knees as he

studied Otskai. "What could convince her to return to her people?"

After Elan translated, Otskai's gaze turned uncertain. At last, she shrugged.

But Adam pressed on, still focused fully on Otskai. "The chief said you might be able to help us. Did he mean help find the Shoshone village? Or help us convince your cousin to come back with us?"

As Elan spoke the words in her tongue, Otskai's face cleared of expression. Almost like Meksem's did at times. This must be a special skill all the Nez Perce people were taught.

When Adam held her gaze, Otskai finally relented, much sooner than Meksem would have. "I don't know the way to the village."

So...a *no* to Adam's first question must mean a *yes* to the second.

Caleb studied Otskai with a new perspective. She and her cousin must be close for the chief to think Otskai was the only one who could convince her. Had they grown up together? Most likely. He could imagine this woman as a young girl in twin braids, huddled close to a friend and whispering secrets.

How many things had the cousins shared? Both pleasure and pain, surely. When they were older, had they whispered of secret loves? Had her cousin been the first person Otskai told when her husband first proposed?

Pain squeezed in Caleb's chest. Maybe the Nimiipuu braves didn't propose the way the young men did back in the states. His belly churned at the thought of Otskai moony-eyed over a man.

But she *had* been married once. Her pretty face still looked so young, too young to have born the weight of all she'd endured.

Adam reached for a twig from the ground in front of him and fingered it as he glanced at Otskai again. "So what think you? Would you like to come with us? You and your son?" He glanced around the circle. "We've plenty of hands to help with him."

A new hope wove through Caleb's chest. Wouldn't it be something if she agreed? Adam spoke as if he assumed their entire group would go.

And they all likely would. Joel and Elan had stayed behind from their last adventure, mostly to let Joel heal from his injuries. And it had been a good opportunity for him to get to know Elan's family since he'd planned to marry her.

But now, he had a feeling Joel wouldn't be left behind again. Nor Meksem, if the determination on her face meant anything. Beaver Tail and Susanna seemed to have settled into married life on the trail.

That left himself and French. Both of them were perfectly unattached, ready to lend a hand.

That thought had never soured his gut before like it was doing now. He'd come on this trip for that very reason—to see new lands, find adventure, and help where he could. Just because the men he'd come with were finding the women God planned for them didn't mean his own intentions had to change.

He glanced at the woman who still hadn't answered Adam's question. The thought of her accompanying them made the journey so much more appealing. The mission would likely take several weeks—weeks when they'd be thrust in close quarters with long days on horseback.

But when his gaze dropped to the lad shoveling a final handful of meat into his mouth, his resolve wavered. This journey could possibly be dangerous for the boy. Yet wasn't the child in danger here too? River Boy seemed to find a way to reach trouble even in this village.

At least on the trail, Caleb could help keep him occupied. Teach him some things. Take him in his saddle for a good part of each day and give Otskai time when she didn't have to bear sole responsibility for her son. They could all help.

He leaned in to grab the woman's attention. "We'd like you to come. We'll all help. Make your work easier. Whatever you need, we'll be there." As Elan quietly translated, he kept his gaze earnest.

Otskai gave no sign of what she might choose. Finally, she gave a single nod.

The tension eased from the air like the release of a long-held breath.

Across the fire, Susanna's voice sounded bright. "Well. Now that that's settled, let's eat."

∽

A WEEK they spent gathering provisions. And it gave Otskai too long to regret her decision.

The times she worked with Elan or Susanna to cook and prepare foods for the journey reminded her how much she enjoyed the company of other women. And Susanna seemed open to teaching her English. Elan too, although she was just learning to grasp the language herself. As the three of them worked together, they all helped keep River Boy busy. The time was a welcome relief from her own constant struggle to keep the boy occupied.

The thought of being near Caleb throughout the journey held more appeal than she was ready to acknowledge. Especially when she glanced at the fence he'd built that made containing her son so much easier.

But all the other times, when it was only her and River Boy, she wanted to retract her choice to accompany this group. As she scraped the hides she'd been drying through the winter, the magnitude of what she still had to do to keep the pelts soft would overwhelm her if she allowed it.

And when she and her son rode her mare along her trap line, the thought of keeping River Boy contained day after long day in the saddle made her want to cry.

Besides, who would check her traps in her absence? She would have to ask one of her cousins, but giving away the carefully selected location of each one felt like wasting all the hard work she'd spent finding those perfect spots.

Not only were furs vital to keeping the two of them clothed and replenishing their supplies, she used them to trade for what she couldn't grow or catch. There was no way she could do all the hunting and fishing necessary to feed herself and her growing lad, but trading provided what they lacked.

Now, she would have to entrust it all to others and lose the bounty the traps would reap during her absence. The loss wasn't worth the few weeks she'd be gaining as a break in the monotony of her work, the few weeks of help in keeping up with her energetic boy.

But she'd given her word, and it would be nice to have Watkuese back. She'd been the only daughter of the aunt and uncle who raised Otskai. In truth, she'd been Otskai's only friend.

The week passed, and Otskai waffled about her decision until the day came to set out.

She tied the last bundle containing the clothing River Boy would need, then hoisted the packs over her shoulder and reached for her son's hand. "Come. We go." Those last two were new words Susanna had taught her in the white man's tongue, and River Boy seemed to pick them up easily.

"Go." He toddled toward her and wrapped his pudgy hand around her finger.

After a final glance around the lodge to make sure she'd not forgotten anything, she led her son through the doorway. Several horses stood outside the fence, one of them her dappled mare. Caleb stood on the horse's far side, adjusting the saddle. Her heart leapt at the sight of him.

Otskai worked for the new word she'd learned. "Hello."

Susanna had said that greeting could be used in any situation, so hopefully this morning would be suitable as well.

The man looked up with the grin that always brightened her spirit. It also gave him a hint of a boyish look, despite his impressive height and broad shoulders. How many winters was he anyway? She'd been cursed with a face that looked far younger than her twenty-two winters. But if his didn't lie in the same way, he was probably only a few winters older than she. Perhaps twenty-five or twenty-six.

"Morning." He spoke the word in a tone of greeting, so maybe that was the better thing to have said in this situation.

He pulled tight the strap he was fiddling with, then stepped away from her horse with a pat on the mare's rump. When he spoke next, the only word she could understand was "pack." He held out his hand with a friendly expression, so he must be reaching for the bundles she carried.

She'd planned to tie them on herself, but he clearly wanted the supplies. Perhaps he had a specific plan for how to order things. Her husband had been that way, and she'd learned quickly enough to go along with what he asked.

She handed the bundles over, and he set to work strapping them behind her saddle. At least that gave her the chance to settle her son in the cradleboard she would tie on her back. The lad squirmed when she tucked him in. He was nearing too big to be confined like this.

But she'd have to use the carrier on this journey. He would be too hard to manage otherwise. Her son would settle once they were on their way. Surely.

A rope of anxiety twisted around her belly. This trip was probably a very bad decision. But it was too late to back out now.

At last, she had him fastened in and hoisted to her back. Standing with the load was tricky, and climbing atop the horse would be even harder.

When Caleb seemed satisfied that her packs were tied securely, he stepped back and reached for the horse's reins, motioning for her to mount. But as he studied her, the line marring his brow showed concern.

She placed her foot in the stirrup and prepared to spring up with enough force to lift her load. Caleb moved around behind her. She couldn't understand what he said, but a glance back showed he was preparing to hoist River Boy as she climbed up.

She wasn't used to having help like this. In truth, she'd rather do it herself, even if getting on the horse took several tries.

But would he be angry if she sent him away? The last thing she wanted was to irritate anyone in this group, especially since they would be traveling together for so long. Better to let him help, at least once. If he made the effort harder, she could motion him back.

But with Caleb lifting her son, his efforts boosted her as well, propelling her into the saddle in one smooth motion. River Boy loosed a giggle as they settled. While she gathered her reins, she sent a glance at the man. He watched her son with a grin so earnest, his pleasure couldn't be feigned.

Finally, he stepped back, still watching her boy. Then he shifted those smiling eyes up to her. He raised his brows in question. "All set?"

She sent him a tentative smile. She wouldn't have thought the answer would be yes…but it was, and she spoke the word in his tongue.

"Yes."

CHAPTER 4

Caleb kept an eye on the woman and boy as their first day in the saddle progressed. He'd started out in the middle of the group, with Otskai a couple horses in front of him. But as the lad seemed to grow bored in the cradleboard on his mother's back, Caleb moved up behind them.

At times he rode side-by-side with Joel, but when they had to move single file, he nudged his mare behind Otskai's. This way, he could make funny faces and try to keep the lad occupied. The boy seemed too big for the pack, and by the time they stopped for the midday break, he was fussing and tugging at the ties over his shoulders. His little legs needed movement, not to be held in the confines of the wooden base. Perhaps she would allow Caleb to hold the lad in front of his saddle for the second half of the day.

After the boy scarfed down the small bites of food Otskai offered him, Caleb kept him busy with a game of hide-and-go-seek around the boulders beside the trail. Soon, they'd added tag into the game to give River Boy a chance to run. His balance was surprisingly good for a tot who couldn't be more than two years old. He must walk over uneven terrain often.

At last, when the others were preparing to mount up, Caleb scooped up the lad and jogged with him to Otskai. Meksem stood with her horse nearby, so he motioned for her to help translate. He kept his gaze casual as he focused on Otskai. "Can the boy ride with me a while? I'll hold tight to him, I promise."

While Meksem translated, River Boy squirmed in his arms. Caleb sent a well-placed tickle to the boy's belly and was rewarded with a giggle that filled the air with so much joy, no one could be sad in the face of it.

Then he turned his focus back to Otskai for her answer. Her expression had softened as she watched her son, love brightening her eyes. Something about the sight made him want to step closer and slip his hand around her. To be part of that tender moment.

He snipped the desire with a quick internal knife. He was only helping with the rambunctious boy, just like he'd promised.

Otskai didn't meet his gaze but glanced at Meksem as she nodded. "Thank you." She spoke the words in English, but was clearly looking at Meksem when she said them. Somehow, that action felt like a slice.

After all, it wasn't Meksem who would be entertaining the boy. But maybe Otskai was just shy. She always seemed quiet in his presence, but he'd sort of thought that was the language barrier. Was she uncomfortable around him?

That thought brought a new pang. He worked so hard to be likable. To be the kind of man others enjoyed being around. The fact that this woman, whose favor he craved more than he should, didn't feel comfortable in his presence stung like a slap to his face.

He forced a pleasant expression, even though she wasn't looking at him to see it. "All right then." He spun the boy quickly enough to gain a smile, then added an extra bounce in his step to turn the lad's toothy grin into a giggle. "We'll have fun, the two of us."

And they would. Though leading a congregation was no longer the way Caleb served the Lord, ministry at an individual level was. And this little fellow would be his main focus for now.

∽

OTSKAI KEPT an ear tuned to the conversation behind her. She could pick out a few words here and there, but it was her son's babbles that eased the knot in her spirit, little by little. At least half the afternoon had passed by now, and she'd finally been able to settle in and enjoy the freedom of riding by herself without worrying over the boy.

At least, not much worry. He'd been her sole focus for so long, her mind and body didn't seem able to relax without that constant undertone of anxiety.

But every time she glanced back, Caleb had a tight grip around her son's belly and was bent low, pointing at something along the trail. River Boy might not understand many of the man's words, but he'd begun to answer after a while. Sometimes just a steady babble. Sometimes repeating what Caleb said in the cutest tones.

At last, she'd been able to adjust her focus to her surroundings, only keeping part of her mind tuned to their voices.

Elan and Joel led their group for now. And Otskai rode just behind them. Elan was familiar with this area, and it helped to have her nearby to translate if Otskai needed her.

They hadn't entered the mountain country yet, surrounded only by rolling hills. She'd suggested they travel southward, skirting the Bitterroot range, since those peaks would still be covered in thick layers of ice. This ride would be longer, but the horses would have fodder, and the nights wouldn't be nearly so cold.

There was one considerable downside to this route, but she'd kept it to herself, for it probably would only bother her.

This trail contained many rivers. And they'd all be at their deepest with melt from the mountain snows.

An image flooded her mind, one from long ago—churning water, foam spinning as the rushing waves swirled around rocks. A weight pressed hard on her chest, and she sucked in air with quick pants.

She grabbed the saddle to hold herself secure and squeezed her eyes shut, willing the memories away. But the darkness of her eyelids only brightened the images, so she flung her eyes open.

Working to slow her breathing, she took in deep inhales of the late-winter air. Bits of snow still piled around the rocks and the sheltered bases of trees. But for the most part, winter grass spread along the valley they were riding through. Soon, the brown would turn green as new shoots brought life to the land.

A rushing murmur worked itself into her awareness, rising above the squeak of saddle leather and the click of horse hooves against stone.

She scanned the land ahead of them. Valleys often meant creeks in this part of the country. But hopefully it would only be a small one, just enough to water the horses.

The dark line of a bank appeared ahead, but she couldn't get a good look at the water until they were almost upon it. Large for a creek, but the horses would be able to walk through without swimming. She exhaled a long, slow breath, pushing the tension in her chest out with the spent air.

Thankfully, her mare didn't possess the same fears Otskai did. After waiting until Joel and Elan's horses finished drinking, she nudged her mount into the water and loosened the reins. As her horse gulped eagerly, Caleb's horse stepped in beside hers.

"River." Her son's happy voice drew her focus to them, and

she did her best to mask her nervousness from being so close to the water with a smile.

The boy reached down for the water, but Caleb's strong arm held him fast in the saddle. Just now, she was more than thankful he had the job of containing the boy instead of her. His squirming would make her own fears so much worse.

Her horse continued to drink. How thirsty could the mare be? She glanced at the man and boy beside her to distract herself again. Her gaze honed on Caleb's hand wrapped around her son's side. Such a large hand, as wide as two of hers. But it fit his massive frame. Fit his nature, strong and protective. That hand could likely do anything that its owner set his mind to.

Her mare shuffled another step forward, and Otskai tightened her grip on the saddle. At last, the horse raised her head, and Otskai nudged her forward to the opposite bank.

At last. Safety.

Caleb's arm had long ago fallen asleep with the lad leaning against him. But at least the boy had worn himself out.

When Beaver Tail signaled a halt to camp for the night, Caleb reined his mare in, as did the others. What should he do with the boy, though? Otskai slipped from her horse, dropping the reins for the mare to stand tied, then turned toward Caleb. Or rather, toward her son.

She reached up for the lad, her gaze on the sleeping face. She still seemed hesitant to look Caleb in the eye. Had he done something wrong? Or maybe he really held no importance to her, at least not compared to her son. Which was the way it should be.

Yet that thought didn't settle well either.

Somehow, she managed to keep the boy asleep as she took him and laid his head on her shoulder. Caleb shook out his arm, then slid to the ground. "Want me to get out a fur to lay him on?"

When she didn't answer, he glanced over at her. Confusion lined her brow. Of course she hadn't understood what he'd said.

He touched the fur wrapping the outside of his pack, then pointed to the ground, then pressed his palms together and laid them against the side of his head like a pillow.

Her face eased into understanding, and she nodded, a grateful smile tugging at the corners of her mouth. Something about the expression cut away all his grumpiness, and his own smile came easily.

As he laid out a buffalo hide, he couldn't help trying to analyze what it was about this woman that affected him so. She had the power to brighten his day like sun peeking through a rain cloud. Yet just by avoiding his gaze, she'd soured his entire evening. No woman had affected him like this since… Well, since his mother.

And he wasn't about to go through that tempest of emotion again. Not for anyone.

After Otskai took the things she needed from her packs, he led her horse and his own to water them in the trickle of a creek near their camp spot. This brook was small enough it likely ran dry in the summer months and only filled with water in the spring from the melting mountain snows.

Adam, Joel, and Beaver Tail had brought the rest of the horses to water. French would be gathering firewood, and the four women would handle fire-making and preparing food.

Caleb scanned their herd as the animals gulped water. "Our group's getting bigger." With pack animals, they'd brought thirteen horses on this journey.

The six of them who had first crossed the Bitterroot Mountains on their westward journey hadn't ridden the spotted Palouse ponies so famous for their endurance. But since then, Adam, Susanna, and Joel had all exchanged their mounts for these native horses, leaving only three of the plain mounts.

Caleb stroked his bay mare's forehead. He wasn't quite ready to get rid of Bessie. She'd been with him since he first set out to start his preaching days. She was the only one who'd stood by him as he slowly failed the flock in Indiana he was supposed to have been tending.

Bessie had been faithful to him, so he would be faithful to her. Although there were times he was pretty sure dragging his monstrous hide up a mountainside was the opposite of the kindness he meant to show. Those were the times he usually got off and walked beside the ol' girl.

Dark had settled on them fully by the time the horses were tied to graze, the fire was established enough to release a roaring heat, and the food passed around. At least they weren't pushing as hard on this trip as they had the last journey. On that mission, they'd ridden through the night to catch up with the braves who'd stolen Meksem's sister. This time, they could start setting up camp before dark and get a full night's sleep.

Yet Caleb's spirit was too restless to settle just yet. He'd already polished off his dried elk meat, so he scooped up the baked camas root and pushed to standing. "Think I'll go for a walk."

He strolled along the little creek. Thankfully, there weren't many clouds to cover the moon and stars, giving him enough light to maneuver rocks and brush. The icy chill in the air kept him moving, but it also kept his mind from lingering on questions he wasn't ready to ponder.

After a few minutes, voices drifted to him, and he paused to listen. Those weren't sounds from their group. Someone else was traveling these parts, and their voices drifted from up ahead.

He'd better find out if they were friend or foe.

CHAPTER 5

Caleb crept forward, but it was almost impossible for his big frame to move with stealth. As the voices grew into distinct sounds, he slowed to decipher words. The rolling cadence wasn't English, but it wasn't the high-low sounds of the Indian dialects either. More like the sweeping tones of the French boatsmen who he, Joel, and Adam had traveled with up the Missouri on the first part of their journey.

They'd met the man they called French in that group, and he'd immediately stood out from the others. He possessed the same lively personality and penchant for storytelling as his countrymen, but he had a seriousness too. A depth of character and faith that had drawn Caleb from their first conversations.

Should Caleb stride forward and introduce himself to these strangers? Or go back and let the others know, maybe bringing French back with him to meet them. He might be needed as an interpreter.

Better the latter choice. Just in case these men didn't take kindly to the presence of a stranger, he should let the others know what was happening. Not that he judged men without giving them a fair chance, but he'd also learned the value in being sensible.

Once he'd traveled far enough away that his footfalls wouldn't be heard by the strangers, he lengthened his stride to cover ground. When he neared their camp, he called out to let the others know it was him, then stepped into the ring of firelight.

Beaver Tail was standing as Caleb scanned the group, the man clearly at the ready in case of danger. Maybe something in Caleb's call had alerted him.

"You're back sooner than we expected." French studied him with a lazy gaze from where he lay back, propped on his elbows. The man kept an easy-going façade, which was part of his charm. Especially with the few ladies they'd met along the way. Including those now part of their group.

Caleb directed his words to French. "Found some people about ten minutes' walk from here. Only got close enough to hear they were speaking French. Thought I'd come back and get a translator before introducing myself."

French sprang to a sitting position, his attention clearly pricked. "How many? Did they speak to you? What are they doing out here?"

Caleb raised his brows. He must not have listened past the word *French*. "Don't know without my translator." He waved the man up. "Come on."

French bolted to his feet and was striding forward as Caleb sent another look around the group. "I suspect they're friendly trappers. We'll say our howdys, then be back."

Beaver wore a look that meant he was thinking hard about something. In their early days together, the man's face had been almost impossible to read. But Caleb had learned to watch his brows and the tilt of his eyes. Now, the man was probably debating whether they should even alert the strangers of their presence.

Caleb met his gaze, keeping his expression relaxed. "I would expect they're friendly."

Beaver's response was a single slow nod. The man would likely be keeping an extra watch tonight. Sleeping with one eye open, as French liked to joke. That was Beaver's way.

Caleb turned and had to step lively to catch up with French. They walked in silence until the hum of voices sounded ahead.

French's stride faltered, and Caleb slowed to see how the man wanted to approach. "Better let them know we're coming so we don't get shot." French's voice was barely loud enough to reach Caleb.

Then he straightened his shoulders and gave a hard stomp over a dry branch. That crack would surely sound their coming. After another couple steps, the voices ahead quieted.

They kept walking, and French called out something in his native tongue. More silence responded, and Caleb brushed his wrist against the knife strapped at his waist, just to make sure it was still there. He didn't have the skill of Beaver Tail or Joel, but he could wield a blade if his life was in danger.

As they neared a cluster of leafless trees, he could just make out the forms of men on horseback through the branches. French spoke again, and finally an answer came from the strangers. Caleb had learned a few French words from their journey upriver, but maybe his ear had gone rusty, for he couldn't decipher what that fellow said.

French motioned him onward as they stepped around the trees to reveal themselves to the group. He set off a rapid-fire speech, motioning toward Caleb as he threw out the words *Caleb Jackson*. Then to himself, *Jean Jacques Baptiste*. With a final flourish as polished as if it were a bow, he finished his monologue.

There were three strangers watching them with expressions more stayed than French's. They didn't seem quite as eager to meet a fellow countryman as did the grinning man standing beside Caleb.

The one mounted on a palomino spoke, using the rolling cadence that made the French language so beautiful, or so the women who'd flocked around the French boatsmen had said. For his part, Caleb preferred to take the measure of a man's inner strength, not rely on the smoothness of the tongue he spoke.

Despite the fact that these three didn't look so friendly, he was willing to give them a fair chance.

French and the spokesman from the other group batted words back and forth for a few minutes, then French turned to Caleb. "They're trappers from the north. From the Northwest Fur Company."

That would be a mark in their favor in French's mind. He'd never said exactly why he despised the Hudson Bay Company so, but he would only associate with men from Northwest Fur.

"They want to meet the others in our group. I believe they mean us no harm."

Caleb's gut tightened. He wasn't sure about bringing strangers around the women and boy. Why had he brought French for a full conversation with these men? Better if he'd just nodded to them in passing and moved on.

But one glance at his friend's expression reminded him why. French was probably missing that camaraderie only someone with the same language and customs could offer. It would be worth a night of extra watchfulness for his friend to have this pleasure.

Hopefully, the strangers wouldn't ask to share their campfire until morning though. But then again, if they left quickly, French wouldn't have as long to enjoy their presence. After all, the Lord had made these strangers as well. He loved them just as much as every single one of His creations. How could Caleb do otherwise?

So he nodded. "Tell them to follow us."

As he and French led the way back to their campsite, French bandied words back and forth with the newcomers. That left Caleb time for his mind to wander ahead. Maybe he should get to the camp early and warn the others of their visitors. But Beaver Tail would be expecting them, no doubt. He would have them all on their guard.

As firelight and smoke drifted from ahead, French cupped his hands around his mouth. "We bring visitors. Fellow countrymen who wish to break bread with us."

Truly, Caleb hadn't seen French so eager in months. Maybe not in the year and a half since they'd left the boatsmen on the Missouri. How had Caleb not realized the change in his friend? Did French regret coming with them? Was he miserable around so many foreign people?

As they made introductions, it turned out the man who'd done most of the talking, Minard, spoke a little broken English. And all three knew some of the signs common to the Indian tribes. The men seemed friendly enough, although more reserved than the boatsmen Caleb had known. Perhaps their quietness came from spending so many months in this remote mountain wilderness.

After French told the shortened version of their journey upriver, then across the mountains to the land of the Nez Perce, and now the purpose for their visit back to the Shoshone, the men listened with keen interest. French did a decent job of speaking so all could understand—first in French to the visitors, then in English so the rest of them would know what he was saying. Even Otskai seemed to hang on his words as she worked to decipher them. She'd moved in front of the fur where her son still slept, shielding him from view by the strangers. Smart lady.

After finishing the highlights of their own story, French asked the men about their travels. Minard spoke only in his mother tongue, and after a few minutes, French raised a hand to pause the fellow as he interpreted for the rest of them. "He says they came down from Rupert's Land, west of the Canadas. They've been following the rivers south, first to Blackfoot country, then along the eastern side of the Bitterroot range. They plan to go north again when the weather warms."

French turned back to the man and asked another question Caleb couldn't decipher.

While the stranger spoke, Caleb used the opportunity to study the two who hadn't added much to the conversation. The smaller man seemed to be merely listening and following what was said with his gaze. But the other man, the one who carried a bit more paunch around his waist, seemed to ignore the speakers completely. He'd studied Beaver Tail for a while, then Joel, then his gaze lingered overlong on Adam. Adam's orange eyes always caught people's interest at first.

But then the stranger turned his focus to the women.

Or rather...not all the women. Just Susanna.

As long as Caleb watched the man, he didn't once flick a gaze toward Elan, Meksem, or Otskai, as though they weren't sitting here around the fire. Did he think them less than the rest because they were native to this land?

He locked his jaw to hold in the anger building in his chest. He knew better than to jump to conclusions. He knew better than anyone that people weren't always what their outer appearance seemed.

But the longer Caleb studied the man, the more the gleam of lust as he studied Susanna was impossible to ignore. Susanna gave the man no notice.

Beaver Tail did though. The hard glare he kept focused on the stranger left no doubt. The fellow seemed not to notice the flaming arrows shooting from the Blackfoot warrior's gaze.

BT might be levelheaded and wiser than most, but his protective instincts soared when it came to his woman.

Perhaps it was time the strangers moved on to find their own campsite for the night.

As soon as the newcomers finished the food that had been passed to them, Caleb found the first gap in conversation. "It was awful nice to meet you fellas. Reckon you'll be wanting to go find a campsite where you can spread your bedrolls and hobble your horses."

French turned to study Caleb, clearly surprised at the barely-veiled suggestion his new friends leave.

Caleb tried to send him a warning glance. French didn't seem to understand, but he must have trusted Caleb's reasons, for he gave a hesitant translation of the invitation to leave.

Even with the honey French probably coated over his words, the strangers' faces darkened as they took in the dismissal. The man who'd been watching Susanna turned downright sullen. But they all three stood.

French rose to see them off, and Caleb did too. The manners Mrs. Sandifer had pressed into him were too deeply ingrained to keep from offering a final farewell and—

He barely stopped the *good riddance* from forming in his thoughts. *Sorry, Lord. Help me see them through Your eyes.*

After a wave, Caleb stood beside French to watch the three mounted forms fade into the darkness. French eased out a long sigh that seemed to push away all the air around them.

Caleb should say something to let him know he understood the pain of longing. The yearning for companionship. For someone who felt familiar. Someone who felt like home. "I guess it was nice to revisit a bit of home, huh?" Those words weren't as profound as he'd been hoping for, but it was a start.

"*Oui.*" The statement came out on another long breath.

Then French seemed to pull himself back together and straightened, turning toward the group a dozen steps behind them. "Guess it might be good to turn in early tonight."

As they took their previous places around the campfire,

Beaver Tail stood and pulled Susanna up by her hand. "Think we'll take a walk." The steel edging his tone almost made Caleb chuckle. The man would be reestablishing his place with his wife, no doubt.

As the pair slipped away, Caleb slid his gaze to Otskai. She stared into the fire's dancing flames, her mind clearly somewhere distant. Was she thinking how the man's lack of attention made her feel less? If only he had the right to take her hand and restore her confidence the way Beaver Tail had with his wife.

If only.

CHAPTER 6

Another day in the saddle, and Otskai was determined this one wouldn't be such a challenge to her emotions. She'd keep her son with her and enjoy the ever-changing scenery.

This time, she would try Caleb's method, planting her son in front of her in the saddle instead of in the cradleboard at her back.

The trail they followed wove up into the mountains, making them ride single file for much of the day. She used the opportunity to practice some of the white language she'd learned. If she set her mind to it, by the end of this journey she could have a decent grasp on the foreign words.

Her son would have the advantage of knowing both tongues from the very beginning. By the time they all returned to their saddles after the midday meal, she'd found a rhythm with everything they passed. "Tree. *Teulikt*." She reached out to touch the barren fingers of an Aspen beside the trail.

River Boy did the same, and when his pudgy fingers struck the branch, he giggled and popped it again.

She pointed up to the wide expanse of blue above them.

"Clear sky. *Aikát.*" Always the white man's tongue first, then the Nimiiputimpt.

"Kat." Her son's version of the Nimiipuu word pressed a smile in her chest.

"Aikát. Clear sky." This time she swapped the order. Her lad was a smart one. He would pick up on the words quickly.

A few times, she turned to Susanna behind her to ask the white man's word for things she didn't know. She hadn't realized how much she'd already learned. If only she could recall the words when she was trying to speak to others.

Especially Caleb. When he drew near her, all speech seemed to flee her mind. Even her own language.

Maybe when they stopped for camp this day, she would be able to face him with confidence. And with her new vocabulary.

A rustle ahead made her mare's ears perk, and Otskai honed her gaze on the path before them. They were working their way down the side of the mountain, skirting around its edge so the trail didn't grow too steep. All she could see in front of them was a cluster of boulders and a gathering of cedars near the base.

But the farther they rode, the more distinct came the rustling. There was no doubt what the sound had to be—she'd heard it so many times in her nightmares.

A river lay somewhere in the valley below.

Not a shallow stream, but quick rushing water swirling around rocks, flowing high against its banks. Infused with melted snow from the mountains.

She gripped tighter on her mare's reins and had to force herself not to tighten the hand secured around her son's belly. She had to stay calm. Maybe this river would still be shallow. Her horse could simply walk across.

But as they rounded that clump of boulders and the trees extended down the mountainside to form a line, she caught her first glimpse of rushing water through their barren branches.

Fear clutched in her chest, stealing a breath. She focused on steady inhales. This fear would take no more than that single breath. She could manage, even if her horse had to swim. She was a grown woman, not a child so easily tossed about by rushing water. Not like she'd once been.

More importantly, she had a son to protect. She couldn't let the river steal her from River Boy as it had stolen her parents from her.

For her son, she would keep a level head. She would bravely do whatever she had to do to get them across. Calmly.

She kept her mare tucked right behind the horse in front of her. Caleb's horse, as usual. The man seemed to have appointed himself as her helper. A fact she both begrudged and was grateful for. As much as his assistance lightened her own load, she should be able to manage by herself. It shouldn't be such a relief for someone else to step in and help.

But just now, she couldn't think about her weakness. If she kept her gaze on the swishing tail of his bay mare and focused on taking steady breaths—each one no shorter or longer or deeper or shallower than the last—she would have the strength she needed for this battle.

With her focus honed, her gaze following the swishing tail, her mind measuring every breath, she couldn't have said how long they rode. Or even where they traveled.

A river? Not in her tiny world. Only the swish of the tail and one perfectly even breath after another.

"Otskai?"

The call of her name broke her concentration. She had to blink to readjust her vision and lift her gaze.

Caleb had turned in his saddle and was watching her, brows raised as he waited for an answer. He'd stopped his horse, although the mare's tail still swished, which was why Otskai hadn't realized their halt. A glance around showed everyone else had stopped too.

They stood at the bank of the river.

Her gaze pulled to the swirling eddies, the bubbles churning around rocks, the water foaming in angry waves.

"Otskai." This time, it took the combination of her name and Caleb riding in front of her line of vision to wrench her focus from the awful clutch of the river. He stopped in front of her, his brows drawn together as his troubled gaze studied her. "What is it?"

She knew that question in his tongue because Elan had taught her to ask it when she needed to know the white man's word for something. And she didn't have to wonder what Caleb wanted to know about now.

It's fear. Out-of-my-mind terror that the water will grab me in its clutches, swirl me around, strike me against rocks, and yank me into its depths. I won't ever return this time. The blackness will hold me down forever, just like it did my parents. The need for breath will drown me in its pain.

But she couldn't say that, even if she'd known the words. She had to force herself from this place. Had to find her strength again.

She focused her mind on steady breaths like before. She honed her gaze on him. His eyes were a dark blue, like the clear night sky just as the sun was almost ready to give up its vivid colors. That blue spoke of his steadiness, his surety. This man was a rock who would hold her up even when the water tried to pull her under.

If she let him. But this line of thought could be almost as dangerous as the other.

River Boy squirmed in front of her, giving her the perfect distraction. She dropped her chin to look at her son.

"Otskai?" Again Caleb called her name, but this time she didn't let herself look up to find his eyes.

"Yes?"

He paused, probably waiting for her to explain the tempest

that must have shown on her face. She wouldn't, even if she could.

When he spoke again, she was able to decipher the words "we" and "river." He motioned toward the water, but she didn't let her gaze follow his arm.

She didn't need another look to know what he was saying. They would have to cross here. In this place of the raging river.

His next words didn't find a home to rest amidst her swirling thoughts. But when he reached out to take her son, his meaning was clear. He would carry her lad to safety on the other side.

Yes. Even as the word raced through her, her mind yanked it back. Hadn't she determined she would do this herself? She had to keep River Boy close. If her parents had only kept her with them, they all would have survived that awful long-ago day. She had to keep her son with her now.

She drew her back straighter and shook her head. "I will." There. She'd even found the white man's words to answer him.

He didn't say anything else, simply sat watching her. She couldn't bring herself to see what his expression would say. Just busied herself settling her son.

At last, Caleb turned his mare away, and the murmur of voices around her lasted for several minutes.

Thankfully, River Boy gave her much to focus on. Now that they weren't moving, the lad had begun to squirm. She returned to their game of naming things but couldn't find the white man's words for anything she pointed to. The Nimiipuu names would be enough for now.

Finally, the horses reassembled in the same order as before, and as Beaver Tail led them onward, her chest pressed tight again. She forced her attention back to the swishing tail in front of her.

This time, not even focusing on steady breaths was enough to keep the edges of her vision from grasping at the churning water as Caleb's mare stepped into it. The first step covered the horse's front ankles, but the mare didn't balk in the least. Maybe the river wasn't as tumultuous as Otskai had expected.

Two more steps, and the mare's back hooves stepped into the water. The ends of the tail were caught up in the flow, swirling downstream.

Her own horse reached the water's edge, and Otskai's effort to keep her breaths steady failed her. No air could pass through the solid stone of her chest.

Her mount followed the others into the river, and Otskai gripped her mane with a tight clutch.

River Boy squirmed, reaching for the water. Otskai tightened her hold. If only she could speak a soothing word to him. But her throat had closed completely.

As the mare stepped fully into the water, her son's wriggling increased. He cried out and pushed at her arm wrapped around him. She fought the urge to draw him tighter. But her hold was probably too constricting already.

A few more steps brought the water up to Otskai's toes. She sucked in a hard breath at the icy touch.

River Boy loosed a cry, stealing a bit more of her confidence. She must be holding the lad too tight, but she couldn't force herself to loosen her hold. In truth, her arm no longer moved as her mind instructed. Her entire body seemed disconnected.

With her mount's next step, the horse tripped, plunging its chest down into the water.

A scream tore from Otskai's throat before she could stop it. She gripped the horse's mane and reins with one hand and her son with the other. River Boy's wails grew louder, but she could do nothing to calm him.

Her horse scrambled for its footing but couldn't seem to find a hold. Another lunge forward, and the water rose up to Otskai's waist. Her son's lower half was submerged, and for some reason that lessened the volume of his cries.

Her own body screamed as fear pressed harder.

Her mare still hadn't found its footing but was lunging forward. Was she…swimming?

A new wave of terror crashed into Otskai as water washed over her, sweeping her legs away from the horse's body with a ferocious shove. The river's current swung her legs downstream, and she clung to the horse with one hand, squeezing her son tight with the other.

Shouts sounded around her. And screams—were those her own?

Terror pushed her down, washing the water over her face, stealing her breath. She swallowed a mouthful of the icy river. Her son cried, but she could only hold him tight. If she lost him in this fierce current, he would be gone forever.

My love. My life. She couldn't lose him. The river fought against her grip on the horse, and those slippery threads of mane slipped from her clutch. But she held fast to the reins.

Her son. *Don't let this be the end.* If only there were a God who could swoop down and pluck them both from the violence of the river, like an eagle clutching its prey in strong talons.

As the water clogged her nose, filling her mouth and gagging on its way down, she could do nothing except cling to her boy and the leathers. Maybe yet the horse would find solid footing and drag them out.

But how could that happen? The river was too strong. Not even her faithful steed could withstand the water's power.

She would die in a watery grave. Just as her parents had. But in her case, her son might die with her.

CHAPTER 7

Caleb reached Otskai's mount with one strong swimming stroke. With a grip on her saddle, he reached out and grabbed Otskai's wrist where she clutched the reins.

The water had sucked her under, and she'd dragged the boy down with her. The current was strong, but not so strong it should have overtaken them like this. The other horses were easily managing to swim across, and Caleb thought he might have been able to press a flat foot to the river bottom and still keep his eyes above the surface.

Yet he'd seen the fear in Otskai's gaze before they'd started out.

Nay—that was terror. Sheer immobilizing terror.

Why had he let her cross by herself? And with her son? He'd known better. His spirit had fought against the choice to let her go alone.

Hadn't he learned by now that, when his heart tugged that strongly, it wasn't his spirit but God doing the leading?

He pulled Otskai to his side, raising her face up out of the water. She still gripped tightly around her son's belly, and the lad rose above the surface with a shrill cry. Otskai looked barely conscious, her head rolling to the side. Her eyes stared with a glassy sheen. He adjusted his hold around her waist, gripping tighter to the saddle with his other hand to keep them upright.

Then his foot struck hard ground at the same time the horse's did. *Thank you, Father.* He kept a hold on the saddle for the first few steps until the water sank below his waist. Then he loosed the horse and used both arms to hold the woman and boy.

She didn't seem able to walk, or even straighten her legs underneath her at all. It was as if she'd fallen under a spell. Sunk into a fear-induced haze.

He shifted his hold and scooped her up and carried her like a babe in both arms. She still held her son but finally loosened her grasp enough to let the lad turn and sit on her belly, his back against Caleb's chest.

As much as Otskai seemed to fear the water, the lad adored it. Now that he wasn't half drowned, a smile dimpled his cheeks, and he rubbed the moisture from his eyes with pudgy fists. Even with gallons of water dripping from them, the woman and child together barely weighed as much as a full sack of flour.

He carried them the last few steps out of the water, where Beaver Tail met him and helped lower the pair to the ground.

Otskai rolled to her side, and her son scampered off her.

"Hey, there." Susanna swooped in and grabbed the boy, lifting him to her hip and out of the way. She would help the lad however he needed.

But Caleb couldn't stop the weight of his worry as he focused on Otskai. She'd pulled her knees up to her belly, curling even smaller. Her shoulders had begun to shake.

Warm. She needed something dry to wrap around her. "Blankets."

But before he could turn to get them, Elan's voice sounded. "I'll bring them."

Caleb dropped to his knees beside Otskai and rested a hand on her quivering shoulder.

But then the shivers turned to jerks, the heaving kind that meant she was about to cast up her accounts. He helped her lift up as water spewed from her mouth. Wave after wave, more than her tiny belly could possibly hold.

How long had she been under? He'd spun around to check on them the moment he first heard the boy's cry. He'd seen her slide off the mare, the current pulling her downstream. He jumped from his own horse that very moment and swam for her.

He realized quickly that, with the strength of the current, he would need to hold onto her horse, so he'd corrected his course. She must have been gulping river water that entire time.

At last, her convulsions stopped, and she draped limply where he held her shoulders up off the ground. He eased her down to rest her cheek on clean grass.

"Blankets." Elan dropped down on Otskai's other side and started to spread one of the coverlets over her. That would help, but Otskai really needed to be cocooned in them. Swaddled like a newborn babe.

"Here." He held out his arms like when he'd carried the woman. "Lay the blanket across me."

Elan seemed to catch his meaning, for she spread the covering over his arms. Beaver Tail and Joel stepped close and lifted Otskai onto the blanket, and Elan wrapped the sides around her, then laid a second blanket over her.

With the woman securely wrapped, Caleb sat and cradled her close. The heat from his body could help her too. Elan tucked the coverings around Otskai's head and feet until the only part exposed was her face.

Otskai's eyes had stayed closed throughout, and her shivers had returned with a fierceness. Her lips were an orangish-blue, an awful color when they'd been so vibrant only an hour before.

He tucked her even closer, wrapping his warmth around her. The others were busy working, setting up camp from the looks of things. It was only an hour or two earlier than their usual stopping time, and Otskai needed a hot fire.

Susanna was tugging a new tunic and leggings on River Boy, making the lad smile with a game of peekaboo. The child had begun to shiver too, but Susanna knew what to do. She wrapped her own soft white wolfskin coat around him, then cradled him and began walking. The lad wouldn't have stayed still if she'd tried to sit with him, but she was smart enough to keep moving as she wrapped him tight.

After long moments, Otskai's shivers finally subsided. He'd tucked her head under his chin, so he couldn't tell if her eyes were open. She must be awake though. Had she finally pulled out of the trance that had seemed to overwhelm her? He didn't dare move to see.

In truth, he was enjoying her nearness too much. She fit so perfectly in his lap, snuggled in his arms. She wasn't stiff as if she were uncomfortable. So relaxed. It felt almost like she trusted him.

And that felt like the best gift she could have offered him. This woman who seemed so young and fragile but carried the weight of so many burdens. And managed them well, despite the challenges her adventurous boy threw her way.

She always seemed so strong. She needed this chance to let herself rest under the strength of another. This yearning building inside him might not be good. But with her in his arms, he couldn't find the desire to fight it. He wanted to be the one to shelter her every time, to lend his strength when hers grew weary.

Yet that should be God's place. He had to do a better job of pointing her upward. If she tried to rely on Caleb Jackson, she would be disappointed every time.

~

WATCHING Susanna play with Otskai's son always raised a warmth in her chest. Like now, as the pair sat in the shade of a leafless Aspen. Susanna held River Boy on her lap, singing some kind of counting song as she wiggled his fingers to the rhythm.

Her boy sat comfortably in the crook of Susanna's arm, a smile on his face as he watched the woman's every move. The bump of Susanna's own babe could just barely be seen beside River Boy.

A longing she hadn't felt in a long time seeped through Otskai. A yearning for another babe to cradle. A playmate for her lively son. She would never have another little one unless she chose to marry again.

But she wouldn't. When her shock over Motsqueh's death had settled, she knew in her heart that if she could possibly manage on her own, she would build a life for herself and her unborn child without the help of a man. She'd never had the chance to make her own choices before that.

Now that she had a taste of freedom—both the liberty of having nobody else to answer to and the challenges of having no one else to rely on—she couldn't bring herself to imagine giving over her independence to another.

Otskai refocused her attention on the soup in the pot before her. Elan had determined they needed this warm stew after that awful river crossing. Since they'd camped early, they had time to prepare a hot meal. While Otskai tended the pot, Elan worked camas root and dried berries into cakes to cook in the coals.

Meksem approached with her hands full of something she'd brought back from her hunt. "I have fox meat to go in the stew. I need only to cut the good parts from the bone." She spoke their Nimiipuu tongue, even though Susanna was close enough to be part of their conversation if they spoke the white language.

Meksem must have used Nimiiputimpt for Otskai, for these two Nimiipuu women had already become fluent in the white man's tongue. They even seemed to prefer it, or maybe speaking it every chance they could was how they'd become so adept this quickly.

She should do the same, no matter how hard the effort was. Knowing the white tongue well would help her with so many of their people coming across the mountains.

And she would be able to speak with Caleb. To understand his words to her. Yet she couldn't let that be her reason. Couldn't let him hold such a place in her heart.

Still, she worked to find the right words in the white tongue. She could only summon a few, so she mixed in some sign language. Maybe that wasn't cheating too much.

She motioned to Meksem, then into the stew. "Meat in pot."

All three women looked her way, and Susanna managed to send a smile without interrupting her song.

Elan nodded and answered using white words, as well. "Your English is very good."

Otskai knew most of the words Elan spoke, but one of them was unfamiliar. "English?"

Understanding danced in Elan's eyes. "That is the language our white men are speaking. There are many tribes among the white, like the many tribes in our land. Caleb is English. Adam and Joel are Spanish, but they speak English now. French is from Canada, and you heard him speak the French tongue with those other men. He speaks English when with these friends." Thankfully, Elan had switched to Nimiipuutimpt for that explanation, or Otskai would never have understood it.

But a new comprehension slipped through her. It made so much sense that the whites would have different tribes, just like those with darker skin. Did they war among each other also?

She ran the word *English* across her tongue, fitting the

sounds so she would remember how they should be spoken when she needed them.

Caleb was English. Something about knowing that made the language even more intriguing for her.

Elan turned and translated for Susanna what she'd just said to Otskai. Amazingly, Otskai understood much of what she said. It helped that she knew the meaning already, but she *was* learning.

The knowledge brought a new sense of power. Just like when she'd finished her camas root harvest and knew she would have enough not only for herself and her son to last through the winter, but extra to trade for what they needed. That way they would never be destitute. She had the power of the camas root fields her parents had handed down to her. With her own hands she could develop her business of trading to provide everything they needed and more.

And now, she was gaining more knowledge of the English tongue.

"Most of the meat is ready." Meksem stood with a hearty portion of sliced fox meat in her hands.

"Here." Otskai motioned into the pot. She'd withheld adding any other meat when she heard Meksem would be hunting. The woman seemed to always come back with fresh game. This fare would be so much better than elk or salmon that had been smoked or dried.

As Meksem bent low to ease the meat into the simmering soup, she seemed to wobble.

Otskai sent a quick glance to her face, and the woman had blanched three shades paler than normal. Her cheeks were rosy, though, with a color that tightened a knot in Otskai's belly. "You're not well."

After emptying the meat into the pot, Meksem stepped back. She seemed to straighten much slower than usual, as though some part of her ached. Probably her entire body if she was taking ill. "I'm fine." She didn't meet Otskai's gaze, and she looked so weary. Yet her voice was strong. It probably took effort to make it so.

"Meksem." Elan was studying her now too. "You do look ill. Clean yourself from the hunt and lie down. Maybe rest will help. And a bit of stew once the meat cooks."

Her mouth parted into what she might have meant as a smile, but the weariness tugging at the corners of her eyes turned the look into a grimace. "I guess I will."

As Meksem gathered her knife and the remnants of the fox carcass, Elan and Susanna refocused their attentions on what they'd been doing before.

Otskai tried to do the same, but she couldn't help a glance into the stew pot at the meat floating in the broth. Would any of what Meksem had handled carry the sickness?

She'd have to let the stew boil overlong to make it clean. River Boy seemed to catch every little ailment those around them had. And the last thing they needed was her son to be ill and cranky.

CHAPTER 8

Otskai had never seen a sickness overtake a person as quickly as Meksem's illness came on. By the time the men returned from the horses, she had finished washing in the river and lay curled under several layers of furs.

Adam's gaze sought her out the moment he neared the camp, and his features formed a frown when he saw her.

He dropped to his knees beside Meksem's pallet and eased down the fur partly covering her face. Otskai couldn't hear what he murmured to her, nor what Meksem said in response. But she didn't miss the quiver in the woman's voice. Her body was racked with shivers.

"Elan?" Adam's voice rose high and tight with worry.

Elan brushed the food crumbs from her hands and rose. "I'm here." Her voice was so soothing, its gentleness would allay anyone's worries. She padded over beside Adam and dropped to her knees by Meksem's head. "I put some water on for a willow bark tea to help her fever. What else is hurting you, Meksem? The tea will help with pain too. Should I add some bear root?"

Otskai had seen Elan warming water but hadn't realized she was already preparing a healing drink for Meksem. She should have known, though. Elan seemed to have the instincts to offer care or kindness when it was needed most.

Otskai was the only mother in this group, so she should be even better equipped than Elan to care for illness. Yet, she couldn't seem to think ahead to what might be needed.

But then a memory slipped in on that thought. Elan had once mentioned she'd lost a child. A girl. No wonder she possessed such a strong mothering touch. A soothing nature.

She paused her stirring to hear Meksem's response but couldn't make out the words.

Elan's answer came clearly though. "I'll brew them both then. And you should eat the stew when it's ready. It will give you strength to fight away this illness."

Otskai returned to her stirring. The sooner the stew was ready the better. But then Elan's next words gave her a new pause. "We should ask God to heal her."

Pray...to the great spirit? Did Adam believe in that being too?

Otskai had never fully embraced the beliefs her uncle and most of her people held. She'd never seen evidence of the great spirit, nor had she experienced any of the visions the others claimed. Maybe the power of the sun god was real for them, but she'd learned after her parents died that she had to make her own way. When she allowed others to plan things for her, she had no control over the outcome.

Like being promised to Motsqueh when she was barely eight winters old. She'd spent her next ten winters living in her aunt and uncle's lodge with the weight of that contract bearing heavy on her. It had been almost a relief when they finally held the marriage feast. Motsqueh hadn't been unkind when she'd lived in his lodge, but she'd felt more like a servant than a wife. Being under his rule had been not much different than when she'd been under the domain of her aunt and uncle. Well...maybe it had been a bit different.

Adam's voice broke through her thoughts as he knelt beside Meksem, and Otskai listened hard to make out the words she could understand—English words. Not just those of the white man.

He must be praying, for he seemed to be petitioning someone for Meksem's health to be restored. A glance back showed his head was bowed, and Elan's too. Yet Adam's tone wasn't anything like the way the shaman pleaded with the great spirit. It sounded almost gentle, as if he was speaking with a good friend. He must be praying to the God of the white man.

Was that who Elan had meant, as well? Had she forsaken the beliefs of The People when she married? Meksem wasn't married yet, but would be soon. Had she also taken on Adam's beliefs?

The other men had gathered around the fire now, all watching Adam and Elan pray. But as Otskai glanced at the men, they weren't just watching, they too had their heads bowed. Caleb's lips were even moving as though in silent petition. Did they all share the same God then?

Curiosity wove its way through her. She wanted to know so much more about their beliefs. She'd always heard the stories of the white man's God, but they seem so far-fetched, she'd not given them much attention. Most of her people believed that the God the white man served was responsible for their wealth, the many guns and beads and tools they carried with them.

But what else did this God do for them? Could he even heal them? If He could give wealth, He must be able to do a great many things. Was He stingy with his favors or generous? So much she didn't know. And the more time she spent around these people, the more she craved answers.

Otskai took over meal preparations as Elan focused her attention on caring for Meksem. They finally got her warm, but she seemed so weak. Almost impossible to believe when the woman had been hunting that very afternoon.

As Otskai moved between the stew pot and the camas cakes, Susanna ended the game she'd been playing with River Boy. "We'll do it again later. Right now I need to help your mama with the food."

Otskai tensed. Keeping her son occupied and away from the fire was one of the best ways Susanna could possibly help. She motioned the woman away. "No." She had to search for the English words, but she finally managed them. "I am fine. You play."

Susanna stopped in her efforts to rise. The baby inside was growing large enough to make movements like that harder. Her gaze searched Otskai's. "Are you certain?"

Otskai nodded. "Play." She motioned toward the lad, who was scrambling back onto Susanna's lap. She didn't quite manage to hold in her grin. Not only was her son safely contained and happy, she'd actually managed a conversation in English.

She reached for the spoon to stir the stew as Caleb rose and moved around the fire toward her. He was such a big man in every way. His height, the breadth of his shoulders, the kindness in his eyes—all so much greater than she was accustomed to.

He dropped to his knees beside her, his presence even larger than the space he filled. "I've stirred a few stewpots in my life. I'd be honored to take over this one. You just tell me if I'm doing it wrong." He reached out his hand toward the spoon, proving that she hadn't misunderstood his words.

Though his meaning was clear, his motive was impossibly murky. Men didn't help with the cooking. Not any man she'd ever been around. They watched. They talked. They waited. They didn't stir the stew.

Yet Caleb still sat with his hand out, patiently waiting for her to hand over the wooden spoon. She finally did, and his big hand brushed her fingers in the transfer. The touch shouldn't unnerve her, since she'd been sitting in his arms only a little while before while she'd regathered her wits after the river crossing. But something about this contact sent a chill all the way up her arm and through her core. Turning her focus to the camas cakes, she pulled several away from the flames and replaced them with more that needed to cook.

Caleb took up steady stirring, and apparently he wasn't as affected by their nearness as she was, for he managed to begin a conversation as well. "How's our fellow now? All warmed up from the river I see."

In Susanna's lap, River Boy looked up from the counting game they'd resumed and sent a beaming smile to Caleb. "Fingers." He held up a hand and wiggled his fingers.

"I see that." Caleb chuckled, a rich rumble that sank around her like a warm blanket. "Do I have fingers too?" He raised his hand and wiggled it the way River Boy was doing.

With a squeal, her son launched himself toward Caleb. Susanna hooked the lad with her arm just in time to keep him from sprawling.

"Ho, there." Caleb raised a staying hand. "You better sit still for now, away from this hot fire. See if Miss Susanna has fingers."

River Boy grabbed Susanna's hand that was wrapped around his belly and pried two of her fingers up. He sent Caleb a broad grin. "Fingers."

Otskai couldn't have held in her smile for anything. Her son had warmed so quickly to these people, grinning more than she'd ever seen him. Susanna had become like a favorite aunt, and Caleb... Well, Caleb was better with the lad than any man she'd known.

She dropped her gaze to the last of the camas cakes she was forming. Her focus had a tendency to find the man even when she told herself not to watch him.

But Caleb's voice drew her back. "I've never been much of a cook, but I love to watch others at work."

She dared a glance to see what he was looking at.

Her.

His gaze shifted from her hands working the food and up to her face. His eyes caught hers, holding them fast even when she tried to pull away. A twinkle resided in his dark blue depths, lifting her spirit in that way Caleb always seemed to manage.

"Those look mighty good. What's in them?" He had mercy on her and dropped his gaze as he nodded toward the cakes she'd already pulled from the fire.

Her insides felt a little bubbly as she followed his focus. She pieced enough words together to know what he was asking, but answering would be another feat. "Camas." She struggled for the English word for *berries*. Had she heard it yet? Her mind couldn't find even a hint, so she plucked one of the partially smashed dried berries out of the cake she was forming. Holding it up in her palm, she spoke the Nimiipuu word. "*Temánit.*"

He leaned forward to see better, and before she realized what he was doing, he plucked the half berry from her hand. His big fingers, with only stubs for nails, dwarfed the tiny half-raspberry. Yet he was gentle as he scooped it up.

Raising the berry on his fingertips, he repeated the Nimiipuu name. "*Temánit.*" He had the sounds right, but his unusual cadence tugged a smile from her.

The light in his eyes turned to a sparkle, which was her only warning before he popped the berry in his mouth. He sent her a wink that slid warmth all the way through her.

This man. How had she let herself turn so soft in his presence?

Throughout the next morning, a hush lay over the camp as Meksem slept. They went through the normal ritual of breaking their fast, but all kept their voices low so the woman huddled under the furs could rest.

Meksem usually wore strength like a comfortable cloak, so this illness that had laid her low must be powerful indeed.

Otskai managed to keep her son quiet as she filled his mouth, but when he'd eaten as much as he would, he started squirming to get up and play. Between the fire in front of them and the river not twenty strides away, the dangers for her son were too great to allow him to wander.

Caleb brushed the crumbs from his hands. "How about I take him to find some birds?" He watched her, waiting for her answer.

She let herself sink into his gaze, just for a moment. His reassuring warmth. Then she nodded. "Thank you."

His grin told her she'd spoken the right answer. In English. She ducked back to the dishes she was cleaning to cover her smile.

"Come on, fella." Caleb gripped her son's hands and lifted him to his feet. Then he held out a finger for the boy to wrap it with one of his chubby hands. "Let's go find some birds."

"Find bird?" River Boy's little boy voice repeated Caleb's words with the sweetest cadence. He tottered along beside the big man, his short legs taking three steps for every one of Caleb's.

"They sure are sweet together." Elan smiled, her gaze following them as she stacked bark plates.

"They are." Otskai let herself watch a moment longer as the pair headed toward a group of trees. River Boy had latched onto Caleb's attention as if he'd been craving it all his life.

Did Caleb know how important he was becoming to her son? A burning clogged her throat as she thought about what it would be like when he left. Would River Boy cry? Probably. Would he soon forget? How could anyone forget this gentle giant? This man who used his strength to help others.

That thought would only keep her shackled to pain, so she pushed it away and focused on wiping the pot they'd used to fry the last of the fox meat. French had taken his morning food with him on a hunt, so maybe he would find more fresh game for the midday meal.

"I'm in need of a few herbs for my healing kit. When we finish here, Joel and I are going to see if we can find some of them along the bank." A smile tickled the corners of Elan's mouth, though her gaze was focused on her work. She and her husband likely wanted time alone even more than fresh herbs. Beaver Tail and Susanna had already slipped away for that same purpose.

Otskai made a shooing motion. "Go now. There's not much left here, and I need something to keep me busy."

Elan paused and gave Otskai an uncertain look. "Are you sure?"

Otskai smiled at her. "Go."

She set her stack of plates aside and stood. "I'll go get Joel then. He, Adam, and French are with the horses." She sent a glance toward Meksem's sleeping form. "Call for Adam if you need anything."

A nod seemed to be all the assurance Elan needed, for she grabbed up her healing pack and started toward the place the animals had been tied to graze.

As Otskai focused on her work again, an old memory slipped through her. The one time she and Motsqueh had gone for a walk alone, the day before their wedding feast.

She'd only seen him from a distance before that, although she'd known she was betrothed to him much of her growing up years. That knowledge had made her a little afraid of him, if she were honest with herself.

Or perhaps not fear… Well, maybe it was fear.

Not that he seemed cruel, but he was a grown man already, more than twelve years older than she was.

He'd come to her that day as she'd been working over the cook fire with Watkuese. When he asked her to walk with him, of course she'd agreed. If they were to join together, she should at least be able to speak to the man.

He'd asked her questions as they walked, and she managed short answers. Yet she couldn't recall now any of the things they'd said.

The only thing she could remember was the feeling like she was being interrogated. Over time, she became used to his pointed manner, and speaking with him became something she didn't have to think about—though she never truly spoke her mind. Motsqueh might not have liked some of the things she said. He always wanted things to be the way he planned.

His home. His hunts. His squaw.

She'd understood that from that first walk, though she'd not thought of it that way until they were married for several moons.

When he was home, she had to abide by his will. But when he was away on his hunt, she could plan her own days. She loved having the time alone. Yet, that wasn't the way a good wife should feel. The independence had always been tinged with guilt.

Now, she had the freedom to live her life as she wanted. If she wasn't perfect, she had only herself to answer to.

Yet the weight of responsibility for her son—especially his safety—carried its own kind of controlling power.

CHAPTER 9

𝒶 noise sounded behind Otskai, pulling her out of her memories as she worked. She turned to see that Meksem had shoved the covers away from her face and upper body. Her eyes were open, though they didn't spark with their usual life. Her face was still pale, but at least the flush of fever no longer marred her cheeks.

Otskai wiped her hands in the grass, then reached for a cup. "You look like you're feeling better. Can you drink water?" Elan had set aside crushed willow bark to make a tea when Meksem awoke. Otskai would get that started as soon as she helped Meksem drink something cool.

"Please." Meksem lifted her head, then worked to prop herself on one elbow as Otskai brought the cup to her.

The faint odor of sickness lingered around the woman, reminding Otskai once more that she couldn't spread this illness to her boy. She kept a little distance between their bodies as she helped Meksem hold the cup.

After several sips, Meksem handed it back with the grateful sigh. "Thank you."

"I'll warm stew and more tea. Better to have food when you

drink it so the taste doesn't make you sick." The bark of the willow could make one a different kind of miserable if taken without food in the belly.

By the time Otskai had stew warm and the willow bark steeping in a cup of hot water, Meksem had rolled one of her furs and used it to prop herself.

Otskai brought her a cup of soup first and knelt beside the woman. Meksem reached for the mug, but her hands trembled when she took it, so Otskai kept her palm under the base.

Meksem didn't push her away, just took a small sip. After four drinks, she closed her eyes and eased out a long breath.

Otskai took the cup back for a moment to let Meksem rest, though she needed to eat more if she could manage it.

"Where are the others?" Meksem's voice came out ragged and weak.

After telling where each of their group had gone, Otskai asked, "Should I get Adam?" She would much prefer not to interrupt Elan and Joel's walk unless the need was great. And really, what could Elan do for this woman that Otskai couldn't?

The corners of Meksem's mouth curved, though her eyes remained closed. "No. He's happy with the horses."

Otskai lifted the soup again. "Try to drink more."

The woman managed a few more gulps. After another rest, she drank some of the willow tea. When she'd had all she could manage, Otskai helped her lie flat again.

Meksem opened her eyes a sliver. "Thank you." The words seemed a token of gratitude from this woman who spoke so little. An even greater offering because of the effort speaking must require in her condition. Her eyelids drifted shut again. "I am glad you're with us."

A burn crept up Otskai's throat. This was no idle comment. Yet how could Otskai be anything more to these people than a stranger who might help them accomplish their goal? Maybe that was why Meksem had spoken those words.

Of course. She wanted the tomahawk back, and returning Watkuese to their village was the only way her uncle would give it.

But something in Meksem's words. The tone or…she couldn't grasp what seemed different. The comment felt pure, unsullied by personal desires.

A gift.

∽

MEKSEM SEEMED BETTER by that evening, and Caleb sure was glad of the fact. He didn't want her to suffer, of course, and she'd seemed miserable when she first took sick the night before. That was the true reason for his relief, really. But the very selfish extra reason was that he was exhausted from keeping River Boy busy all day.

He'd never thought a two-year-old could wear him out in the space of an hour, but that possibility had now proved fact.

Over and over.

The boy was cute as a baby bunny, and had an adventurous spirit that would give even Adam a run for his money. But he hadn't yet learned to temper that boundless energy with caution. Which meant Caleb had to be by his side, or at least tagging along to catch up, every minute.

How did Otskai accomplish this every single day with no one else to help? No wonder the boy managed to escape sometimes. Even the most protective of mothers couldn't be as diligent as this lad needed and get anything else done. He was a two-person job, no doubt about it.

Since Otskai had her hands full with him all the time, Caleb had done his best to keep the boy occupied this day. But it was a relief to hand him over for her to feed as they sat around the campfire to eat the evening meal. Susanna had slipped into the place on the boy's other side, so Caleb settled in to watch them from across the fire.

He would've thought Otskai would be refreshed from a day without her chief responsibility, but she must have done too much work around the camp, for the light in her pretty eyes seemed dimmer than usual. Dark circles shadowed underneath them, and even her patience with her son seemed thinner than normal. Maybe something else was bothering her.

If the other women would handle cleanup after the meal, perhaps he could get her off for a walk to ask.

Or perhaps this was her leftover exhaustion from the ordeal in the river the day before. If she sought out her bed directly after the meal, that might give him his answer.

Of course, she wouldn't be able to rest until her son fell asleep. Maybe Caleb could volunteer to lie down beside River Boy. Tell stories or count stars until the chap drifted off.

"Another day in camp should have the horses rested up." Adam's voice cut through Caleb's planning.

The man sent his gaze around their group, as though seeking agreement from them all. He seemed to be ignoring the glare from the woman beside him. Meksem had felt well enough to draw near the fire to eat, although she sat propped against furs stacked behind her.

"No." She spoke with the authority only a warrior could manage. The word hit its mark like a well-placed arrow.

Adam turned her way with an innocent expression.

"By morning I'll be ready to ride." Meksem's half-reclined position didn't diminish the power of her gaze in the least.

Adam shrugged. "There's no hurry. No one's life is at stake this time. Another day to graze will be good for the horses, prepare them for the trek through the mountains."

Meksem shook her head, but her gaze seemed to soften. "Tomorrow, I will be ready."

For a long moment, Adam studied her. A conversation

seemed to pass between them. It wasn't quite as intimate a look as Susanna and Beaver Tail when they both turned sappy. This connection held something more like respect. Well...maybe it was a little sappy, too.

Caleb looked away, his focus quickly drawn to where River Boy was shoveling bits of camas cake in his mouth, smearing it across his chin and cheeks in the process. But even that picture didn't keep him from hearing Adam's soft words.

"All right. If you say so." His tone held nothing begrudging, only an intimacy that brought heat to Caleb's cheeks.

"Did I ever tell you about the time my donkey took sick?" French's voice broke the intimate moment like an ax blade crashing through a paper-thin layer of ice.

Caleb sent a scowl toward the man to show him his comment wasn't timed very well. At least not the glaring tone of his voice.

But French's expression didn't hold the usual grin it did when he shared one of his far-fetched tales. His dark brows had lowered in a look that spoke of frustration. Maybe even a hint of anger. And it was aimed toward Adam and Meksem. Had something happened to draw the man's ire?

French was usually as pleasant and easy-going as a fellow could find. In fact, none of them were of an ill nature. Their group had become a tight family, knitted together by the bond of friendship, honed by more than one adventure where each man's life lay in the protection of the others.

Maybe French was having a bad day. Maybe he was catching whatever had laid Meksem low. That would explain a bit of ill humor.

French looked to be waiting for a response, so Caleb took his bait. "Don't think I've heard that one."

"Well, we were checking traps along the river. I had a bunch that winter, and all were working well, so I took the burro with me to empty and reset them. One day she just laid down there on the bank and stretched out her head in the snow." French's expression had softened, and he seemed to be settling into the story. Though his eyes still didn't sparkle like they normally did when he told a wild tale.

"At first, I couldn't get her up. This was up north in Rupert's Land. The weather had dropped cold enough to freeze a tear on the cheek, so I knew we couldn't stay away from camp without a fire for long. Some winters there could be bad enough to make even the snowshoe hares hibernate 'til spring."

The man seemed to have gained more wild experiences than a fellow twice his age. It was a wonder how he could have done as much as he had in his five-and-twenty years. But then again, their little group had packed enough in these past two years to fill a book—or two or three.

French had paused in his tale, so Caleb leaned forward. "What did you do?"

"Well, I sang to her a few minutes, all her favorites. That seemed to give her enough energy to get up on her feet. Her nose was dripping and her skin overly warm, her head hanging low, so I knew she wasn't her usual self. We made it back to camp, and I let her lie down again by the fire while I heated some caribou stew for her."

The twinkle had finally returned to French's eyes, and he tapped his finger on his knee in the way he usually did just before the punch line. "By the time she finished a bowl full of my supper, the others were back to camp for the night. Rondeau had a bit of brandy he warmed by the fire. The donkey drank it dry, then had a little nap. By the time I woke in the morning, she was healthier than a bright-eyed maiden."

Caleb couldn't help a chuckle as he shook his head. "I'm never sure whether to believe your stories or not, old man."

French pressed a hand to his chest. "Every word is truth, upon my honor."

Caleb raised his brows. "I wouldn't dare question your

honor." And though he spoke the words in a jesting tone, he meant them with all sincerity.

French was a good man, loyal to the core. Caleb had a feeling from a few unguarded moments that there was more pain in French's past than he let on. Maybe that was part of the reason why the man had been on his own at such an early age and therefore had enjoyed so many adventures so young.

Caleb offered him an earnest smile. "I'm awful glad you're with us, Frenchy."

His friend's mouth tipped in a grin that hinted at a bit of the rogue. "Me, too. Most days."

OTSKAI GRIPPED her saddle with both hands as they rode the next day. Meksem had indeed regained enough strength to continue their journey. Most of the color had returned to her face that morning. But by their midday stop, she was pale enough again that Adam insisted they rest in that place longer than usual. Meksem slept for a while, but when she woke, she was determined to press on.

In truth, Otskai had been hoping against hope she would ask to camp. She should've known better with a woman as strong as Meksem.

The night before, Otskai had thought her tiredness had stemmed only from too little activity that day. Her aunt had often said that rest brought on the need to rest more.

Not that she'd been sitting in camp doing nothing, but with Caleb keeping her son occupied, she'd appointed herself the one to stay near Meksem and help with anything she needed. Since the woman slept much of the day, that left Otskai time to work on sewing a new tunic and leggings for River Boy.

By the time she'd finished preparing the evening meal, her body felt so drained she could barely sit up to eat. When Elan and Susanna insisted on doing the cleanup after the meal, she'd accepted their offer. Getting her son to lie down on his pallet took more time than usual, and as she lay with him, she'd fallen asleep before he stopped wiggling.

When she woke in the night to pull on more blankets, he'd been asleep beside her. At least he hadn't wandered to the river in her lapse. She really should have stayed awake with him, no matter how heavy her eyes felt.

She'd not wanted to allow the thought that she could be taking sick, but as the morning had progressed this day, she could no longer deny the chills that made her huddle in her coat.

Caleb had offered for her son to ride with him, and she'd not had the strength to decline. In truth, the man was a gift she would never again take lightly.

Her son adored Caleb and actually obeyed most of his commands. Maybe because they didn't come out sounding like demands. Caleb had a way of suggesting something that made you want to move a whole range of mountains to accomplish it.

Now that they'd been back in the saddle for a while after the midday rest, it was all Otskai could do to sit straight on her horse. Heat rose off her skin in searing waves, and she could barely keep the chills from rattling her teeth so loudly that the others would hear it.

She would not slow them down though. She wouldn't be the weakest member of the group.

Her mouth felt as dry as the surface of the sun. Her lips stung from the heat burning inside her. There may still be water in the leather pouch hanging from her saddle. But with the way the chills shook her, stealing all the strength from her body, if she let go of the saddle, she would topple off. No question about it.

So she clung. Her mind ached too much to think, and her

vision had honed to the swishing tail of the mare in front of her. Caleb's horse.

A feeling like she'd done this very thing before swept through her. And she had. First, a steady breath in. A sharp pain twinged in her chest, but she worked through it with a steady breath out. First in, then out. No gaps between each breath, no hurried intakes. Perfectly measured. Her eyes honed in on the *swish, swish* of the tail in front of her.

She couldn't have said how much time passed. But when her mare's nose bumped the horse in front of her, the side-to-side swish changed to a quick upwards flick.

Otskai blinked, maybe for the first time in a while, if the burn in her eyes meant anything.

She gripped the saddle tighter as she pressed her eyes shut against the ache in her head. Her upper body seemed to sway, teetering to one side. She pushed hard to correct herself, but then she was falling the other way.

Her fingers squeezed tight around the saddle to hold her upright, but the momentum of her body was too strong—her fingers and arms too weak.

She sucked a hard breath as she lost her hold on the saddle. The swimming in her head swirled harder, and she squeezed her eyes shut.

Her head struck first, and she gasped as her shoulder slammed hard into the unforgiving ground.

Then blessed peace took over.

CHAPTER 10

"Otskai!" Caleb leapt to the ground, River Boy still in his arms as he scrambled back to the woman who had just fallen from her horse.

Her mount sidestepped away from her lifeless form.

Caleb set the boy to the side, away from the horses, and closed the final step to drop to his knees beside Otskai's still body.

She lay on her belly, face turned to the side, eyes closed. Had she hit her head? Should he touch her? What in the world would make her fall off her horse like this?

With the gentlest of touches, he laid his hand on her shoulder.

She didn't move, her body perfectly relaxed.

"Otskai. What's wrong?" If only he knew the words in her language. He'd been working to learn, but since they spoke English in camp, the going was slow. He had to ask the meaning of every word he learned. Maybe he should ask their group to speak Nimiiputimpt, at least some of the time.

Elan crouched on Otskai's other side, and thankfully

Susanna had scooped up the fussing boy. No doubt he was worried about his mother.

"What happened?" Elan pressed a hand to Otskai's face. "She's burning up. She must have caught Meksem's illness. We need to make camp and get her comfortable."

As Elan stood and started giving orders to the others, Caleb pressed his fingers against Otskai's temple where Elan had. Heat rose off her like steam from boiling water. How had he not felt that when he touched her shoulder? The thickness of her coat must be holding the warmth in. Maybe that was part of the reason she was so hot, smothering under these layers.

But then a shiver coursed through her body. She stirred, moaning as she seemed to be trying to turn on her side. The moan turned to a mumble.

He helped her shift onto her side, and as more shivers convulsed through her body, she curled her knees up, tucking into herself.

She was freezing, so he scooped her up and settled into a sitting position, setting her in his lap much the way he'd done to warm her after her near drowning in the river.

With her eyes squeezed shut, the lower half of her jaw vibrated as she quivered for warmth.

He tucked her closer, cradling her face in the crook of his neck, rocking to ease her misery. "Shh. It's all right. We'll get you warm. Easy there." He murmured whatever slipped out to calm her as he held her close, rocking her in a rhythm that felt as natural as time. She snuggled so perfectly in the curve of his big body. Just the right size for him to protect her in every way.

If only he could take this miserable sickness from her, soothe away the fever and whatever else was adding to her pain.

The others were hurrying through the makings of camp. Adam, French, and Beaver Tail settling the horses, Joel bringing the packs and dry wood they carried so Meksem could build a fire, and Elan laying out bedding that must be for Otskai. Susanna had taken responsibility for River Boy and was helping the lad unpack pots, probably for the evening meal. Or maybe to make a tea for Otskai like they'd given Meksem.

Normally, Caleb would've stepped in to help where he could, with the horses or lifting heavy things. Maybe toting pots and water skins to and from the creek so the women could start cooking.

But he had no desire to move from Otskai. His place was where she needed him. She'd burrowed so deeply inside him, despite the fact that their lack of shared language made speaking a challenge. Something about her, her need—but not *just* her need—called to him. Drew him.

She was so strong, yet kind and giving of herself. The very first time he met her, the first time they'd come to her camp, she had brought baked camas from her own supply to provide food for them. Then she'd returned later that day with herbs to help Joel and Adam through their injuries and sickness. She'd given her own hard-gained supplies to strangers in need.

And as he'd watched her since then, she never seemed to stop giving. Her lad took up much of what she had to offer, but she still found ways to share herself and her belongings with those around her.

Even yesterday, when he'd been keeping her son busy, she spent much of the day nursing Meksem. And now, that effort had likely brought on this sickness that tortured her.

How could he not be drawn to such a beautiful heart as hers?

Elan straightened from the bed pallet she'd laid out and turned to him. "Bring her here."

Caleb worked to keep Otskai steady as he rose to his knees, then to standing. Her shivers had eased a little, and she seemed a bit more relaxed in his arms. As he shifted his hold on her, he realized she was clutching the neck of his shirt. Maybe to steady herself.

He lowered to his knees beside the furs, and Elan lifted the top layers for him to lay Otskai underneath.

When he pulled her away from his body and eased her onto the soft wolf fur, her hand still gripped tight to his shirt collar. The other hand scrambled along his chest, reaching for something to hold.

"Easy there." He reached for both of her hands with his. "It's all right, Otskai. You're safe. We're going to get you warm."

She gripped his hands with a hold fiercer than he would have thought her slight self could manage. The shivers convulsed her body again, even stronger than before.

Elan pulled the stack of fur coverings over her shoulders, leaving her hands peeking out where they clutched Caleb's. Otskai still squeezed her eyes shut, and if her lids were pressed as tight as she was gripping his hands, there wasn't much that would pry them open.

He wrapped his fingers tight around hers, holding her secure in his grip. As her breathing shifted to something more intentional, deep steady inhales and exhales, he rubbed his thumbs over the back of her hands.

"There you go. You're getting warm." He kept his voice calm and soothing, just as if he were speaking to a foal fresh from its mother's womb. A steady tone could ease the fears of any of God's creatures, soothing a racing heartbeat and helping a little thing gain strength to manage what should come next.

"Help her, Lord." He kept his voice the same soothing tone as his words turned to a prayer. "Heal Otskai from this sickness. Jesus gave us the power to bind every evil spirit of sickness, and we use that power now to cast away this ailment." Strength and certainty washed through him as he continued the prayer. Through the power Jesus gave his disciples, this awful fever and whatever else came with it would be gone from their camp.

The prayer consumed his focus for a while, but when he

spoke a final "in Jesus's name," he realized Otskai's shivering had faded completely.

She still held his hands, but not with the tight grip of before. Her breathing had softened, even steadier now, like that of sleep. Had God taken the fever already? Her hands were still warm, but not the searing heat. Maybe this would be enough for her to rest.

He shifted his hold to loosen one of his hands from hers, then reached up to stroke the loose tendrils of hair that had fallen over her face. Her skin held a sheen of sweat, her hair damp around the edges. And though her skin didn't burn with fever as much as it had before, the feel of her soft face under his calloused fingers sent warmth all the way up his arm.

She was so beautiful, he couldn't help taking the chance to watch her. Always before, he'd simply known how her beauty struck him with every glance. But he'd never had the opportunity to decipher each individual feature, how they all worked together to form the whole alluring package.

Her lashes were long and curled a bit at the ends, the curl surprising because her hair lay fine and straight. The bones of her cheeks curved upward at the outer edges, helping to create the heart shape of her face as her chin came to a rounded point.

Sounds approached from behind, forcing his focus away from her. Susanna was coming with River Boy, the lad's hand clutching hers and worry marring the soft skin of his brow.

"He wants to see his mama." Susanna kept her voice to a whisper, and her gaze shifted from Caleb to Otskai.

Caleb motioned the boy over. If Otskai was awake, she would open her eyes for her son, he had no doubt.

But she didn't, and the fur covering her shoulders rose and fell in steady rhythm. Caleb released her hand and reached for the boy, holding one finger over his mouth to help the lad understand to be as quiet as possible.

River Boy crept closer, and Caleb settled him in his lap, then bent low to speak into the boy's ear. "Your mama's feeling a lot better. She's just tired now."

The boy studied Otskai for long moments. Caleb stayed still with him, giving him as much time as he needed. For once, the lad wasn't squirming or wiggling to get free. If only Caleb knew what the child was thinking, he could relieve his fears better.

But for now, all he could do was sit with him. After a while, River Boy turned sideways so he could lay his cheek against Caleb's chest and still watch his mother. In that position, the boy's body seemed to relax.

Caleb held him in a loose hold, praying over him as they sat. That the Lord would bring peace to this boy's spirit and raise him up to know his Heavenly Father. That he would be a strong man of God.

After a while, the gentle rise and fall of the boy's shoulders signaled sleep.

WEARINESS WEIGHTED Otskai's body as she worked to open her eyes. Her head pounded, especially when morning light shone brightly around her. A sparrow had already begun its song. She squinted to make out how late she'd slept—the sun was already a finger above the horizon.

She should rise quickly and make up for her lapse, but her body ached as though she'd spent a full day running through the mountains. And her head…

A noise sounded behind her, and she worked to turn beneath her fur coverings. The activity was coming from Elan and Meksem, who worked by the campfire. But her gaze caught on a figure sitting a little more than an arm's length away from her pallet.

Caleb.

He was watching her, his gaze even warmer than usual in the morning light. "Good morning." His voice soothed over her, infusing her with a bit of strength. It didn't carry the usual morning gravel as if he'd just awakened.

He must've been up for a while. Had she missed the meal? Maybe the others were already saddling the horses.

She pushed the blankets aside and started to work herself up to sitting.

But he raised a staying hand. "Rest. There's no hurry."

The effort to simply prop an elbow under herself winded her, so she stayed in that position for a moment as she worked for English words to ask. "We ride?"

He shook his head. "We rest today."

Were they doing this for her? Nothing in his gaze showed of accusation or even disappointment.

She had only a vague memory of stopping to camp the night before, but couldn't even remember climbing down from her horse. A memory slipped in of fighting the shaking chills though. At least they were gone this morning. "I can ride." Surely once she rose and started moving, her strength would return to her.

He tipped his head, seeming to assess her. "There's no hurry."

She could make out the words distinctly enough—Caleb's speech always seemed easier to decipher than the others—but she wasn't quite sure their meaning. Whatever they were, he wasn't rushing to stand and get moving on the trail.

In fact, he held something in his lap. Something flat she'd not seen before.

He followed her gaze, then lifted the object. It seemed flimsy in his hold, almost like a stack of buckskins. But not.

"I was reading my Bible." He tipped the thing so she could see the flat surface, which was white with lots of tiny black markings. "These are God's words."

God's words? She'd heard of a book that was part of Caleb's people's religion. Maybe now was her chance to ask more.

She lowered from her elbow back to rest against the furs, and her aching shoulder thanked her for the relief. Then she focused on Caleb again as she searched for the right words. "Tell me of your God."

CHAPTER 11

Caleb's heart leapt at Otskai's halting words. This was what he had longed for. Longed for with every person he met, but even more so with this woman.

He knew how to share God's love with others, but like a wave washing over him, the magnitude of her request sank through him. God had used the entire Bible to reveal Himself to His people. How could Caleb manage it in a few sentences? And he'd have to keep them simple enough she could translate in her mind.

Maybe he should ask Elan or Meksem to come over…but perhaps not. He'd learned long ago not to foist more on a person than they were ready to hear. Nothing more than they asked for.

For now, he could begin with the basics. "God made the world, everything you see." He used a few signs to illustrate the words. "He made you and me. All of us. And He sees us." He'd learned more signs than he realized, for he was able to find ways to show everything so far. But this most important part had to be clear.

"He loves us. He cares about everything he made. Has a good

path for all of us." He locked his gaze with hers as he pointed to her. "You too, Otskai. He loves you. Cares about your life. And He has a good plan for you and your son."

Her expression had deepened, twin lines of concentration forming between her brows.

He kept quiet now, letting that sink in. Maybe he'd said too much at once. In truth, that was much of the heart of the gospel. The main part left was to share how God wanted her to open herself to Him. Accept His gift of salvation through Jesus and choose to live for Him.

After long moments, she looked to be searching for words. Maybe this was the time to call Elan or Meksem. But he resisted glancing their way. Otskai could summon them if she chose. This moment seemed too tenuous to break.

At last, she spoke a single word. "Why?"

Caleb leaned in, doing everything he could to express the enormity of what he was about to say. "Simply because He loves you."

She seemed to be absorbing that. But before she could answer, a little boy's voice sounded from the direction of the horses.

River Boy came toddling toward them, his joy evident in the wide smile lighting his face. He spoke a word he'd used in the past that must mean *mama*.

Otskai held out a hand as he charged near, and the boy put his small palm in hers. Even as her thumb stroked across his wrist, she seemed to be holding him off as she spoke a string of Nimiipuu words.

Susanna and Beaver Tail approached in the boy's wake. Susanna already looked a little worn, probably from keeping up with the lad. And maybe that was why Beaver Tail accompanied her now.

River Boy tried to push in toward his mother, maybe for a hug or maybe simply to climb on her, as he liked to do. A splash of pain crossed Otskai's gaze, so Caleb leaned forward and scooped up the boy, spinning him around to face him. "Hey there, fella. How are the horses doing today?"

The boy charged Caleb like he'd attempted with his mother, and Caleb wrapped his arms around the lad, pulling him close as River Boy jabbered something that made not a lick of sense.

"Is that right?" He held him close, soaking in that sweet scent he seemed to always carry. A bit of sweat mixed with something indefinable that always made pleasure clog Caleb's throat.

Maybe that was the aroma of trust. River Boy seemed to offer that sweet gift so freely.

Caleb's gaze found Otskai's. The expression on her face was a mixture of pleasure and something like longing. Did she wish Caleb hadn't snatched her boy away from her? He couldn't let the lad hurt his mother, no matter how innocent the intention. But maybe he could find a way for them to be together without bringing pain to Otskai's weak body.

When River Boy turned in Caleb's arms, Caleb scooted closer to Otskai and settled the boy in his lap. "Tell your mama what we call this." He plucked a blade of grass and held it up.

"Gas." The boy grinned. "*Zikzik.*"

Caleb's brows slid up. Was that second word the Nimiipuu version? He glanced toward Otskai as he repeated the boy. "Zikzik?"

Otskai nodded, pleasure softening her face. Maybe at his understanding, or maybe because he'd attempted to speak her language. How hard it must be to travel with people who always spoke a foreign tongue. At least Elan or Meksem made the effort to translate when their group was speaking. And Otskai seemed to be learning English quickly.

But it wasn't fair for him to put the burden on her. He needed to learn the Nimiipuu tongue. And it was high time he put some effort into it.

For the next hour or so, he quizzed Otskai on the Nimiipuu

words for everything he could think of. He may not remember half of them, but he would do his best.

The others who slipped in and out of camp seemed amused by their conversation. But they weren't making fun. All of them had struggled to learn languages on this journey. His effort may not be as graceful as some of the others', but he would get it one way or another.

When River Boy started squirming, Elan took him for a walk to gather sticks for the fire. Otskai didn't ask again if they would ride that day. In truth, she seemed barely able to sit up until after the noon meal.

But every so often she would send a worried glanced toward the horses. Maybe he should tell her again to relax, but that hadn't seemed to help before. At least she wasn't pushing herself beyond what her strength would allow.

Lord willing, this day of rest would aid both Otskai and Meksem. Then tomorrow they could get back on the trail and finally make progress to the Shoshone camp.

For he had a feeling that the journey wouldn't be the hardest part of this mission.

WEAKNESS KEPT Otskai almost limp in the saddle the next morning, but at least she could sit up on her own. Caleb kept her son settled in front of him, and since the trail was wide through here, the two of them rode side-by-side.

River Boy alternated between chattering an endless stream of barely understandable Nimiipuu words and contented silence. But in both cases, he seemed happy to be perched with the man he'd become so attached to. Never once did he try to climb out of the firm hand Caleb kept around his belly.

Would her son be heartbroken when Caleb eventually left them? A burn pressed her eyes, an emotion she had no business feeling. She didn't have the strength right now to separate the pair and help her little boy guard his heart. The least she could do was guard her own from this gentle man who'd taken a place there so quickly.

When they stopped for the noon meal, she let herself lie in the grass to eat. Her son hadn't slept in the saddle, so he snuggled in beside her. This was the first time she'd allowed him so close, but maybe she was enough recovered that she wouldn't pass the illness on to him.

She could only hope.

THEY SPENT a short day in the saddle on the first day after Otskai's sickness, and by the second morning, she seemed mostly recovered. Meksem, too, had returned to her usual vigor quicker than Caleb would've expected. And thanks be to God, none of the rest of them had taken sick.

In fact, the next few days on the trail were the calmest their little group had experienced in as long as he could remember. The weather held steady with chilly spring temperatures. Snow still covered many of the peaks, but the lower lands were turning the green of early spring. The creeks rushed full of snowmelt, but thankfully none were deep enough to require the horses to swim. He made sure River Boy rode with him or Beaver Tail anytime they waded through water, and he kept a close eye on Otskai during the crossings. Though she seemed edgy, the panic from before didn't cloud her eyes.

He could get used to a life like this. Days filled with this beautiful woman by his side, sharing responsibility for the boy who'd long ago snatched a big part of his heart.

The days were busy, no doubt. But the kind of busy that left a man feeling full and satisfied. He couldn't help the prayer he'd started sending up more often each day. *Let Otskai learn to love me, Father. If these two are Your plan for my life, open her heart to me.*

Surely God wouldn't have planted them so deeply in Caleb's heart if the Lord didn't have a design that included the three of them together.

Yet despite the occasional times he caught a tender glance from Otskai as she watched him play with her son, she still seemed to keep herself distant from him. Not physically, but she wasn't warming to him. Those looks he saw occasionally must be only pleasure at watching her son's joy.

Finding excuses to be near her wasn't hard—she seemed to always be wrist-deep in wash water after meals or slicing food in preparation for the next big feed. He could wash a pot as well as the next man, and he was even picking up a few new cooking methods from helping her. He could only pray he didn't have to use them as a bachelor after this journey was over.

She seemed to appreciate the help and had lost most of her shyness around him. He was doing his best to speak her language every chance he could, but she was also working to learn English. That left a lot of halting conversation, made up of half heavily-accented words and half sign language.

At least they had those moments of connection.

Maybe that would make her more willing to agree when he asked her for a walk under the stars that evening.

As usual, Otskai played a significant role in preparing their evening meal. He would've been happy with cold elk meat and baked camas root, but the women usually outdid themselves with a hot meal in the evenings. That suited him fine too.

River Boy finished eating first, and Susanna gave him a set of sticks to tap with on a rock. They only occupied the lad a few minutes, so Caleb tied a pebble on each end to add more sound.

As the lad pounded the sticks again, a wide, toothy grin split his face. Who could resist a smile like that?

As usual, Otskai began cleanup as soon as she finished her

fare. French and Adam were swapping tales about boyhood pranks.

If Caleb didn't take action, this night seemed destined to end in the way many of them did—him keeping the boy busy while Otskai oversaw clean-up from the meal. The other men would wipe down rifles, sharpen knives, or do whatever else needed doing. Then the couples would slip away, French might check on the horses, and Otskai would take over her son to bed him down to sleep. The problem was, she usually laid herself beside him, and Caleb wouldn't see her again until morning.

If he wanted to find a few moments to woo her, he'd have to make that time himself.

He eased up to his feet quietly so he wouldn't disrupt the storytelling across the fire. Then he stepped nearer to Otskai so she could hear when he spoke quietly. He caught her gaze and used motions, along with what he'd learned of her language.

"I walk with River Boy." He motioned to himself, then the lad, then pointed to a path leading away from the nearby creek. "Will you walk with us?"

Surprise flashed through her gaze. She glanced at her son, then to the trail Caleb had pointed to. Then she eyed the plates stacked in her hands. That last direction probably meant she planned to refuse him. Did she really think she was the only one who could put away the eating supplies? He sent Elan a pleading glance.

The woman took the hint easily and touched Otskai's arm. "Go. I'll do this."

He'd actually learned enough in their tongue to understand those few words. *Thank you, Lord.*

Otskai sent a shy look his way, then rose in a graceful movement. Reaching a hand to her son, she spoke to him in English. "Come. We walk."

The boy stood and followed, although he didn't take Otskai's hand. Not a surprise to Caleb. Since the lad was forced to spend so much time in the saddle, he wasn't much for being confined when he had the chance to move.

Otskai and her son started toward the path, and she looked like she might leave Caleb behind if he didn't take the initiative to go along on his own.

He wasn't going to lose this opportunity.

CHAPTER 12

Caleb walked beside Otskai as they followed a game trail that wove around boulders and scruffy trees. The lad trotted ahead, but his short legs kept him from roaming too far from them. As long as they kept their walk brisk enough.

No leisurely stroll, this.

Still, Caleb was walking beside this beautiful woman, moonlight shining overhead. The nights were still chilly, cold enough to need fur coats, but not so cold their breath clouded around them. Spring would be on them soon, and he was more than ready.

"I must thank you." Otskai's quiet words slipped through the air between them. She spoke English, which was her usual pattern when she began a conversation. When *he* started, he always tried to speak Nimiiputimpt. Both because he needed the practice and because he wanted to do everything he could to make their talks easier for her.

She was learning faster than he was, though, so anytime she began the conversation, he could usually count on their discussion moving along a lot easier.

He'd not expected her to be the first to speak now, but he

couldn't help a bit of relief. He wanted this time apart to be a chance for them to get to know each other.

In answer, he shrugged. "No thanks needed." She probably meant for helping with her son. As much as the boy wore him out, he loved their playtimes. And he loved that Otskai seemed lighter now than she had back in her village. Less weighed down.

She turned to look at him as they walked. "Yes. Thanks needed. You're good with my son. He enjoys you."

She motioned toward the boy, who was coming toward them, bringing something to show. Two pebbles, from the looks of them.

"Nice." Caleb took the stones the boy handed him.

"Rocks." The lad reached for them back, and Caleb handed them over with a grin.

"Rocks. Well done." As the boy toddled off, they resumed walking. "He's learning quickly."

"More thanks to you. I want him to learn English. I don't want it to be hard for him."

He slid a glance at her. "Like it's been hard for you. Yet you're learning much faster than I am. It's clear you do well with everything you set your mind to."

Her mouth tightened, losing any hint of the relaxed pleasure from moments before. What was it she worried about? In her tone had been a touch of... Well, maybe worry for the lad. Maybe she thought she wasn't doing the best for him.

He could set her mind at ease on that account. "You're doing a great job with River Boy." He shifted his gaze from her to check on the boy, who required constant supervision. Yet he kept his mind focused on what he wanted to say, even with one eye on the lad.

"He's happy and healthy and loved. Those are most important." Maybe his own story would help Otskai. He didn't usually tell people about his growing-up years. He'd mentioned his past to Beaver Tail once, though not the details, but hadn't even told the others. Yet if he wanted to get to know her better, he had to be willing to share himself.

"My mama raised me alone. I never knew my father, and she never said much about him. Only that they weren't married. I'm actually not sure he ever knew about me. Maybe she didn't have the chance to tell him before he moved on." Perhaps better not to linger on that part. It didn't matter for what he wanted to say.

"Anyway, she worked hard to make sure we had what we needed. All through my childhood, she worked most of her waking hours. In the daytime she kept shop for a mercantile, kind of like a trader." He glanced sideways to see if she was following his story.

She was watching him with interest and gave a nod that showed she understood, at least most of his words.

He turned his focus forward again. "At night, she worked in a café. Feeding others for payment." He scrambled for a better way to explain it. "Trade for food."

When he glanced sideways again, she gave another nod.

"I didn't see her very much. She was always working. We had a home and food and the things we needed, and I learned how to keep myself busy. But when I began going to school, I started to get in trouble."

Her face shadowed with uncertainty, and he searched for a better way to explain. The school part wasn't important, but his actions were. "I did bad things as a boy. When I was six or seven winters old. Then a man became a friend to me. He was a reverend, one who taught people about God. He took me under his wing, let me visit his lodge, and taught me to do the right thing. He made me *want* to do right."

Otskai's eyes shone with a depth of understanding. An awareness that made her look far older than her years. As though she had lived through something similar. Had she lost one or both parents at a young age? Did she have someone else who stepped into the gap for her? Taught her how to grow into a woman worthy of honor and respect? She certainly had become such a woman, so she must've had someone.

Dare he ask? Even if he could find the words, that wasn't the kind of thing a fellow inquired about. She would need to tell when she was ready.

Her gaze drifted to her son, who'd stopped on the trail ahead, peering at something in a clump of bushes. "I hope my son finds such a man." Her words were barely more than a whisper.

His heart understood them better than his ears.

I want to be that man. And not just a stranger on the outside. But he couldn't say that. Not yet.

Ahead of them, River Boy smacked a bush, releasing a delighted squeal. The branches rustled, more than just from his touch. Maybe the lad had frightened a bird.

River Boy took a step nearer the brush, and Caleb hastened his stride. There was no telling what manner of thorns or branches he might get caught up in.

Caleb was four steps from the boy when a low growl raised the hairs on his neck. His pulse slammed through his throat, and he lunged forward.

Lord, no. Not this. Even as part of his focus stayed on the boy, he strained to see into the quivering bushes.

One more step and he scooped up the boy, then spun to charge back the way they'd come. But before he could carry the lad away, the branches smacked him as a furry mass erupted from the shrubs.

"Run!" Caleb sprinted hard, closing the distance between him and Otskai as a grizzly bear thundered behind them.

They raced back down the trail, Caleb still holding the lad in a sideways grip, his arm around the boy's middle, the head of fluffy black hair pointed forward. He didn't have time to move him into a comfortable position.

The bear's rumbling growls thundered through Caleb's chest with every pounding step. Otskai was running faster than he'd have guessed she could, the speed of her shorter legs more than a match for his longer stride.

But the bear wasn't backing off.

He'd not thought grizzlies would have awakened from their winter sleep yet. This one must have stirred from hibernation ravenous. A hunger those bushes couldn't dull. Only meat could quell it, and this creature lusted for a nice bloodied human steak.

He couldn't let Otskai or the boy get hurt. Nor could he lead the beast back to their camp, although that was exactly where they were running. He'd have to veer away and make sure the bear went with him. But he couldn't take the lad.

If they got close enough to camp, would the others hear and be ready with rifles? Maybe he could throw the boy toward his mother and face the bear. Enough to keep its rage directed toward him. Could the others get a shot in before the creature mauled him into a bloody mess?

He'd have to risk it. That was the only plan he could manage with his heart thundering and grizzly breath heating his neck.

With the only extra strength he could manage, he yelled, "Bear!" Hopefully the others would hear and have their weapons ready.

They were closing hard on the camp now. He could probably see it if he were looking. But he had too much to focus on elsewhere.

Save me, Lord.

He braced his feet to slow his speed. "Otskai! Get the boy." He whipped the lad around and ducked low to send him in a roll. The motion surely wasn't pleasant, but it was better than tossing him on the hard ground, and Caleb had to get him out of the way.

As he suspected, Otskai spun at his words and leapt for her son.

Caleb turned his focus on the bear, whirling to meet the creature. Ducking his head low, he barreled his right shoulder into the massive chest.

Underneath the fur, a hard body slammed into him. A massive paw pummeled the top of Caleb's head. He'd tucked his chin against his chest, else that blow would've struck his face.

But it was enough to knock him backward. He scrambled to keep his footing, but a slam from the other paw shoved him forward, like a ragdoll tossed from one hand to the other.

Pain shot up his neck as his head flopped. He tried to keep himself straight, infuse strength in his body—fight back.

But the bear spun him, then smashed him hard onto the ground. His shoulder hit first, and his head bounced off the packed dirt. Pain ricocheted through his skull.

The ache echoed so long, he couldn't tell if the blast of gunfire had come from within his mind or without.

O*TSKAI SCREAMED* as she clutched her son to herself and ran.

The rifle sounded again, and the explosion made her jerk. Her foot stumbled. Her toes struck a rock and she went down. Her knees pounded the ground first, then her hip and shoulder. She gripped her son tight, pressing him to her chest as she struggled to draw breath.

Was the bear advancing? She craned to see. Her body had lost all its strength to run, but she would summon the effort if necessary to get River Boy out of danger.

In the moonlight, a form lay still, like a boulder rising almost as tall as her waist. There had been no boulder there, so it must be the bear.

The body didn't move.

"Otskai." A loud whisper came from behind her. "Are you hurt?"

She rolled to see the speaker, shifting her son with her. The movement seemed to wake him from the trance he'd been under. He let out a wail.

Susanna crawled toward her.

Otskai glanced back at the bear and caught the movement of a man edging toward the form, rifle raised in a firing position. That outline had to be Beaver Tail.

River Boy was squirming out of her hold, so she returned her focus to him, loosening her arms as she worked to sit up.

"Let me have him." Susanna rose to her knees and reached for the lad.

River Boy crawled toward her as Otskai let him go. Relief that he was safe overrode the ache from the fact that he felt Susanna's arms would be safer than his mother's. He probably just wanted as far away from the trauma of past moments as he could get.

As Otskai worked up to her feet, she glanced back to make sure Beaver Tail wasn't in danger with the bear. With no weapon, she could do naught but scream. But she'd run for a gun if she had to.

The hulking form didn't move as Beaver Tail nudged it with his rifle.

She eased out a breath.

But where was Caleb? She glanced to the left, the direction he'd been running after he sent River Boy to her. He'd been distracting the bear so she and her son could get to safety. But it didn't look like the bear had covered much ground since that last moment she saw them.

A painful suspicion slid through her, and she shifted her gaze to the ground around the beast.

There. The spot where Beaver Tail focused. That wasn't a fallen tree.

A cry loosed from her throat as she stumbled forward. *No!* He couldn't be.

How had the bear caught up to him? But in truth, how could the man have escaped the bear? The creature had been nearly tromping their heels.

That instant it took him to send her son rolling toward her must have been enough for the bear to reach him.

As she neared the form where Beaver Tail crouched, her heart pounded an aching rhythm in her head. He couldn't be. Not Caleb.

She dropped to her knees opposite Beaver Tail and took in the way Caleb's body lay. The moon had ducked behind the clouds as though it couldn't stand to look down on the awfulness below.

Caleb lay with his face pressed to the ground, one arm hidden beneath him and the other sprawled away from his side. His legs extended straight, with one kicked out in front of him, and the other facing a little backward. As though he were a stiff-armed toy a child had tossed to the ground, stuck in the position he'd landed.

She rested a hand on his back, feeling for the pulse of life flowing through him.

A moan slipped from the ground where his face was pressed.

Or maybe she'd only imagined the sound. She leaned over him, resting her other hand on his arm and lowering so her ear was near his cheek. "Caleb?"

His body shifted the slightest bit under her hands.

She rose up, and another moan slipped from him as he started to turn.

Tentative hope leapt within her. He was alive, but she had no idea if he would stay that way.

CHAPTER 13

Otskai helped Caleb turn, first onto his side, then easing onto his back. He seemed to have little power within him to accomplish the movement—not even enough to shift his feet as she turned the rest of him. She moved down the length of his body and lifted one thick leg over the other to lay his limbs out straight. Stretched out like this, this man was even bigger than he seemed standing beside her.

"Where does it hurt?" Beaver Tail was feeling down Caleb's left arm. When he moved back up to the shoulder, Caleb moaned and tried to pull away.

Beaver Tail's hand stilled. "He's bleeding here."

The bear must have struck its claws in the spot. Or perhaps Caleb's bone had broken through the skin. Either would be painful.

As Beaver Tail worked the antler buttons to open Caleb's coat, Otskai placed her hands on Caleb's other shoulder to check that arm.

Her first touch landed on thick wetness. Her belly churned with the sensation. How badly was he hurt? Were these all claw marks?

"Blood here." She kept her voice low and in her own tongue, so maybe Caleb wouldn't understand. Although he surely knew the severity of the wounds better than she did. At least the pain from it.

Beaver Tail gave a single nod to show he'd heard her and finally finished working open the buttons on the coat. He opened his side, and she did the same with hers.

Caleb's breathing grew loud and hoarser, but his eyes stayed closed. Maybe the cold air made the wounds burn, or the shifting of his tunic rubbing against them did.

The moon cast a small shadow on her side, but she couldn't miss the dark lines striating his right shoulder. Claws must have pierced his outer fur as though it were no thicker than water. A glance at the shoulder on Beaver's side showed the same stripes, appearing darker in the direct moonlight. At least the moon had peeked out from behind the clouds to face this awful sight.

"Is there anything broken, Caleb?" Beaver Tail's voice rang clear and measured. "We need to get you back to the fire and cleaned up. There I'll have enough light to take care of any broken bones if you know of them."

Caleb's lips parted, and he seemed to be gathering himself to speak. "Maybe...the ankle. Hurts." The words were no louder than a gravelly whisper.

Realization pulsed through her. She should have known the ankle might be broken when he didn't move the foot on his own. She'd merely thought him weakened from his other injuries, or maybe in shock from the ordeal itself.

Beaver Tail glanced up at Joel, Adam, and French. She'd not even realized they were standing nearby. These comrades seemed as near as brothers, although Joel and Adam were the only ones who bore a resemblance to each other. Behind them a few steps stood Elan and Meksem and Susanna swaying River Boy in her arms.

A thread of relief slipped through Otskai. She could always

trust Susanna with her son. These others too. They'd all taken the place of family for the boy.

And for her? Maybe. At least for now.

Beaver Tail and the other men surrounded Caleb, and she stepped back to give them room as they hoisted him and carried him toward the firelight.

Elan and Meksem had already moved into action, laying out a fur pallet. Otskai forced her feet into motion. She should be the one scurrying around, readying things to help him.

Not that she had a real claim on him. No claim at all, save the way her heart yearned when he was near and the way he filled her thoughts when he wasn't.

After the men settled him on the fur, they stepped back. All except Beaver Tail, who took up the side he'd been on before. While he started working the coat sleeve down Caleb's arm, he glanced up at her, probably wondering why she was still standing there doing nothing. "We need to remove these. Clean the wounds."

She dropped to her knees on Caleb's other side and set in to do as Beaver Tail did.

This time, the light of the fire came from behind her, clearly showing the blood matted in the brown fur of his coat sleeve. The lighter brown of his buckskin tunic appeared through the tears in the outer fur. The red of more blood showed too. She could only hope the layers had protected his flesh, at least from deep punctures.

Caleb's jaw had locked impossibly tight, the cords of his neck flexing at times. He must be holding in a lot of pain. The side of his face nearest Beaver Tail had a spot of blood up by the temple, but it didn't seem to be expanding, so maybe the crimson was merely a smear or scratch.

As gently as she could manage, she extracted Caleb's arm from the coat, and the sight that glared up at her sent the burn of tears surging into her eyes. Long strips of his tunic hung loose down his side, revealing deep bloodied gashes in the skin beneath.

She reached for the bottom hem of the shirt and eased it upward. Beaver Tail helped on his side, and soon they worked the garment up to his underarms. His belly was streaked with so many claw marks, like lashes of a whip with a knife blade tied to the end. She glanced up at Caleb's face, as much to block out the sight of his mangled flesh as to see how he was faring.

His eyes were open now, slitted and focused on her. He surely saw the horror in her expression, and she did her best to wipe her features clean.

She touched the buckskin gathered at his chest. "Need take off." Doing so would require him to shift in ways that would be painful.

"I'll cut it off him." Beaver Tail was already slicing through the leather with his hunting knife. She should've thought of that. The garment was too mangled for repair anyway.

As Beaver worked, she couldn't pull her eyes from the hold of Caleb's gaze. Though his lids were only open enough for her to see their dark rounds, they had locked on her, as though she were his only source of breath. Whatever he needed from her, she would give it.

She reached to brush her fingers across his brow, and the moment her skin touched his warmth, she realized the intimacy of what she did. But the hard lines of his jaw eased with the contact. Somehow, she was soothing a bit of his pain. So she let her fingers roam, brushing down his temple, then resting on his cheek, her thumb caressing the stubble that had grown there for several days.

Beaver Tail finished cutting away the tunic on his side and leaned toward her to do the same on her side. She pulled back to give him room, but kept her gaze locked with Caleb's. Her insides ached so much, it couldn't be just sadness for the pain he was feeling. She longed for something, a longing that would no longer be denied.

Yet she couldn't let herself name that desire. Not now. Not yet.

As Beaver Tail finished and eased away, Elan appeared at Caleb's head with a pot. "Here's water for washing. I put a few herbs in to help with the pain." Something in her voice made Otskai glance up at her. Elan's face had paled more than usual, but her eyes held a grim determination. She must be as worried about Caleb's condition as Otskai was.

Otskai reached for the cloth floating in the pot, then raised it over Caleb's shoulder. She squeezed the liquid out, letting it dribble onto his wounds.

He sucked in a breath, and his eyes squeezed shut, his jaw locking tight again. Beaver Tail moved down to Caleb's feet, probably to look at that ankle. She had a feeling his pain wouldn't be ending anytime soon.

She continued squeezing water over his injuries, watching the diluted blood run off in tiny pink streams. Some of the claw marks went deep, at least as deep as her thumbnail. Some of them may have pierced the sinews beneath his skin, but none seemed to be bleeding in excess.

A glance down the length of his legs didn't show any slashes in his leggings. The bear seemed to have done most of his damage on Caleb's top half. But she had yet to see his back.

Elan had moved to kneel behind Caleb's head and was studying the wounds. A frown drew her brows together. "I have garlic steeping in more water. I think also we should bind the wound with witch hazel leaves. I've seen them help keep claw marks from festering."

The knot in Otskai's chest pulled tighter. Wounds from a bear or wildcat did tend to fester more than most cuts. Sometimes to the point of taking a life. She'd seen that happen twice.

A brave injured by one of those animals would be mending, up and moving around.

Then he would be laid low in the space of a single meal, taken with a sweat that burned the life out of him.

A new rush of tears stung her eyes, and she focused on wringing the last of the drops from the cloth before she dipped it again.

After she'd used the full pot of water on Caleb's front, French helped turn him over while Beaver Tail supported his injured leg so she could get a look at Caleb's back.

With the bloodied tunic pulled away, the same bevy of marks scarred his skin, turning his beautifully sculpted back into a sight that churned nausea in her middle.

As she washed the blood from those wounds, at least one tear slipped past her defenses. She didn't draw attention to it by sniffing or wiping her cheek against her shoulder. Caleb's agony was so much worse than hers.

By the time she finished cleaning him, Meksem had appeared with the witch hazel leaves, and she and Elan helped Otskai wrap Caleb's upper body with several strips of cloth.

They finally had him settled, and every line of him seemed pinched tight against the pain. A few spots on his belly were swelling, although it was hard to tell for sure with the cuts striped in multiple directions across him. She would need to watch those places. If the claws had struck something vital within…

She couldn't let her mind travel that path.

They laid Caleb on his back, and Beaver settled the man's leg straight. "The joint is swelling, but no bone has broken through. While he lies still, I won't wrap it." He sent a weighted look to Otskai, his meaning clear.

If Caleb did attempt to move around in coming days, they would need to do something more to protect the ankle.

She nodded, then reached for the stack of blankets and furs

Susanna had brought. She laid the cloth blanket on him first. Caleb was the only one of the party who used a fabric covering along with his furs every night. And the feel of it might help soothe him now.

This one had grown ragged at the edges, as woven cloth was apt to do. Its top was constructed of many small pieces of fabric stitched together. The blanket had probably once been beautiful, but many of the patches had come loose on one or more sides, flapping as she spread the covering over him.

She fingered one of them. The pieces were stitched with some kind of flexible woven strip, not the quills her people used for beadwork on leather. She would repair the blanket if she could find something that would be as soft and pliant as what was used before. She'd have to think on what might work.

After arranging the furs over the blanket, she scanned the length of Caleb. His wounds were clean and wrapped. Hopefully the coverings would soon warm him. Elan was brewing willow tea to ease his pain and help him sleep. Beyond that, was there anything that might help him?

"We've done all we can." Elan laid a gentle hand on Otskai's back. "Go. See to yourself and your son."

Otskai's gaze roamed to her boy. He was eating again, sitting beside Susanna. His eyes hung heavy, probably the excitement wearing off. She should help him sleep. Assure him they were all well.

But the thought sent her focus back to Caleb. *Would* he be well? If he didn't recover from these wounds, losing him would slay her son. Her own heart might not recover.

She couldn't let that happen. Even though she'd known Caleb would leave them at the end of this journey, that was different from watching him die in agony. She had to do everything she could to keep him alive.

She shook her head in response to Elan. "When the bark tea is ready, I'll feed him. Then see to my son."

"*I* will feed him the tea." Elan's voice came firmer than usual. "You and your son need to rest."

Otskai sent another look to River Boy. He truly did look exhausted. Susanna was an able caretaker, but after the ordeal this night, Otskai should be the one to provide that extra measure of security to his little heart.

Caleb needed her too, but River Boy was her flesh. The one dependent on her alone.

Her heart ached to the point of rending, but she had to make a choice. And that choice had to be her child. Didn't it?

CHAPTER 14

*E*very part of Caleb ached. An ache all the way through his bones, to every callous and toenail. He had to sit up, though.

He'd been watching the others buzz around camp like a group of hummingbirds, working steadily while he laid there with barely enough strength to crack his eyelids open. Otskai and Elan kept plying him with tea, and he half wondered if that was keeping him flat on his back. A position his cut-up skin didn't thank him for.

With most of the others busy working over the bear carcass, he eased himself onto his left side. That arm groaned as loudly as his back had, having to bear his weight on the cuts. Maybe soon he could work himself up to sitting. He was fairly certain he'd spoken truth when he said his right ankle was broken. The foot simply wouldn't move the way he told it to.

How in the world were they going to get to the Shoshone camp with him in this state? Adam had been right the other night when he'd told Meksem they didn't have to hurry on this journey. But that didn't mean they could sit around this place for a week or two until he would be able to stand on both feet.

And if the break in his ankle was a bad one, he'd be lame longer than that.

The others should ride on without him. By the time they found Watkeuse and circled back, he should be well enough to ride. As long as they left him his rifle, his bedroll, some food, and some water nearby, he'd manage just fine.

But he knew better than to even suggest the idea. They'd kept to a no-one-goes-alone policy in every part of their travels. And the stakes had been much higher in some of those other situations.

So, he was back to his first question. How was he going to get himself in good enough shape to be upright in the saddle come the next morning?

He could ride with the injured foot hanging loose—it'd likely be swollen bigger than his head by evening, but he could manage that.

Getting on and off would be a trick. Maybe sweet Bessie could stand to carry his substantial hide all day without relief. That way he wouldn't need to climb on and off more than once. Although it'd be better for the swelling if he could soak the ankle in cool creek water whenever they rested.

Come to think of it, that was something he should be doing right now.

He eyed the banks of the little stream maybe a dozen steps away. Crawling might be a sight easier than finding a stick to help him hobble. And he'd be less likely to draw the attention of everyone working on the bear. They might not want him moving around, but he had to do something. Good thing there were a few cedar shrub trees separating that skinning area from where he lay beside the fire coals.

He managed to work up to his hands and one knee, but he had to clamp hard on his jaw to keep his pain from leeching out in noises that would bring the others.

His ankle raged as if a bonfire flamed inside it, and he had to use his hands to lift his calf and turn the foot into a crawling position. That eased the pain just a tad. This movement might do more damage than any good that would come from soaking the foot.

Should he stop now? Just getting up on hands and knees felt like he'd done half the work to reach the creek. Better keep moving and not waste his efforts so far.

Dragging that foot still ached like a gunshot with every stride, but the rest of his body eased the farther he went. This had been a wise move. Maybe lying around all morning had stoved him up.

He reached the creek, which was barely high enough to cover his swollen ankle. Hopefully, the icy water would still do the trick.

Sitting there with nothing to lean back against was a mite harder than he'd expected. Just that measly crawl had exhausted his limbs. But he'd worked hard enough to get to the water, he planned to stay here 'til his foot felt nigh to freezing off.

Just when lying back in the grass was starting to sound like a good idea, a muffled cry sounded from the direction of camp.

"Caleb!" Otskai's voice, and it weighed heavy with fear.

"Here. I'm here. Down at the water." He waved so she would see him. The last thing he'd wanted was to worry her. He was supposed to be relieving the extra challenges from her load, not adding to them.

She was already marching his way. And though she was usually good at masking her thoughts on her pretty face, there was no denying the anger charging through her stride.

She'd barely covered half the distance to reach him when she started in. "What?" She threw out a hand to take in Caleb's entire location. She'd spoken that first word in English, but now started spouting Nimiiputimpt faster than his ears could catch the words.

He didn't have to understand them though. Anger sounded the same in every tongue.

She was a sight to behold, standing not two strides from him, hands talking as fast as her lips. Eyes flashing and sparking so they shone even brighter than the sun behind her.

He did his best to clamp his teeth on his grin, but the fact that she was this rattled over his wellbeing made it even harder not to smile. He hadn't meant to spark her ire. And he shouldn't be enjoying her anger so much.

Most of the time his mother had been too exhausted to get angry with his boyhood antics. But the few times her temper had flared, he'd learned shying away from her only made the fury grow hotter. Getting close was what cooled the flame.

So now, he reached his hand out to Otskai. The chance she'd take it and let him tug her down beside him was slim. But if this didn't work, he'd find another way to ask.

She eased her firing off, her hands slowing their rapid motions. She spoke her final words slowly, as though they were an afterthought while she focused on determining his intentions.

He reached his hand farther, flattening his fingers to show he wanted her to put her palm on his.

Though her furrowed brow showed she wasn't ready to call a truce, she eased her hand out and placed it in his.

He wrapped his big fingers around her hand and gave a gentle tug. With his other hand, he patted the ground beside him. Her mouth pinched in a reluctant line, but she sank down next to him.

The grin tried to burst out of him, but he locked it inside. He had a feeling concern for him might have been the main reason she complied, and crowing over her compliance would do him no favors.

He didn't release her hand but let their clasp rest in the grass between them. Might be best to distract her, too, lest she dwell on their touch. Besides, he had some explaining to do.

He motioned with his free hand toward his foot in the water. "I thought the cold would help the swelling in my ankle."

That pinch returned to her mouth as she studied his overlarge appendage. His feet had never been much to look at, with his toes so long and the joints too big. He'd not spent much time thinking about his feet before, but maybe he shouldn't have drawn attention to them. Not the attention of this woman, whose good opinion he craved.

But the long release of her breath snagged his focus from that selfish line of thought. He glanced at her as she ran a hand down the side of her face. That was the motion of a woman trying to push off the weight of fear and anxiety.

And he'd been the one to layer that burden on her this time.

"I'm sorry, Otskai. I didn't mean to worry you." The thought that she might get so upset had never really entered his mind.

She met his gaze, and the red lacing the whites of her eyes pierced an arrow through his chest.

"Oh, Otskai." He reached over and cupped her cheek. He should be taken outside camp and hung at sunset for causing this woman grief. But all he could do now was apologize and do better next time. "Forgive me?"

She didn't drop her gaze, but her eyes turned shy. She gave a single nod. "Forgive."

Then her shoulders rose as she took in a deep breath as the look in her eyes turned earnest. "I need say thank you. For giving your life for my son and for me."

Warmth eased the tightening in his chest. "I'm glad it didn't come to that."

His body longed to reach forward and brush her lips with his. That would sure make him feel better, but he had a feeling it wouldn't have the same effect on her. Not yet, but in time, if the Lord willed.

For now, he'd be praying that time came soon. And also, he'd be praying he didn't mess up like this again. This woman's heart was too precious to handle without care.

THEY WERE on the trail again, and Otskai had her son firmly planted in front of her saddle.

She rode behind Caleb when the trail forced them to ride single file, but when the path widened through the valleys, she nudged her mare up beside his.

He slumped in the saddle, both hands gripping the front bar. But at least he stayed upright. His face wore grim exhaustion most of the time, but when he realized she was looking, he usually tried to summon a smile. The saddest smile she'd ever seen. The look tightened her chest every time.

But he was determined they would keep riding. He'd allowed two days of rest after the bear attack but then insisted they move on. He'd spent much of those two days sitting by the stream, keeping his foot in the water until he probably couldn't feel the limb anymore. Then he'd rest it on the bank for a while, then again in the water.

By midway through that second day, the ankle had eased down to near its regular size. And Caleb seemed much stronger than before. Still tender in all his wounds but not so weak as that first sleep.

She'd unwrapped and cleaned the wounds twice each day, applying new witch hazel leaves to keep the cuts from festering. Some of the lacerations were deep in his flesh. They would close eventually, but the scars they left would be bright for years.

Badges of honor. For he'd lived, and the bear had not.

The others had allowed her to attend him, and her heart took too much pleasure in each touch. His bare back, thick with ropy muscles. Those wide shoulders, surely broader than the bear's had been. And his arms, with so much strength. She could still feel the way they'd wrapped her after she nearly drowned in the river. When he cradled her, she'd felt more protected than ever before. So safe. So free from every burden.

Her gaze wandered to those arms now. They bulged with the strain of gripping the saddle. He looked as though that hold might be all that was keeping him on his horse.

She sent a glance skyward. The sun had only traveled half of its downward trek to the west. Not their usual time to camp, but maybe the others would have mercy on Caleb and stop early.

The sound of a horse coming up on her left made her turn. Adam moved alongside as the trail widened. His face showed a purpose. A question.

She waited for him to speak.

He glanced her way. "I traveled with the Shoshone last autumn. Stayed in three different camps. Can you tell me about the people your cousin went with? I might have met them."

She took a minute to decipher the words. Most were familiar, she just had to think of the meanings.

As his question came clear, relief slipped through her. They were only five or six sleeps from the land of the Shoshone, but she'd had no idea how to find Watkeuse's camp, other than asking those they met along the way. If Adam had knowledge of these people, their search could be so much easier.

She sank into the memory of those men who'd come the summer her cousin left. Five braves had approached the edge of their camp, with one woman riding with them, midway between the age of Watkeuse and her mother.

The woman had slept in Watkeuse's lodge, and the two of them had taken to each other from the beginning. Otskai had already been given to Motsqueh by then and had just learned of the new life growing inside her. Accomplishing each day's needs amidst the roiling in her belly had been all she could manage, so she'd seen little of the Shoshone visitors.

Maybe if she'd spent more time with her cousin, she would have seen what was happening and been able to stop it. Watkeuse had never been one to abide quietly under an order, especially when her father issued commands in his domineering manner. Otskai was one of the only people who saw that clearly and always took a different tact to manage her cousin.

Watkeuse hadn't come to Otskai's lodge to say farewell before she left. She'd not told anyone of her leaving. Her father and all the camp knew the Shoshone were to go, and a farewell ceremony was given for them—a goodwill offering to help solidify the tentative peace between their peoples.

Yet when Watkeuse's mother had risen the next morning and the girl was gone, along with the Shoshone, they had no doubt who had taken her.

Her father had gathered a war party and thundered after them. Watkeuse must have expected it, for she met them a distance from those she traveled with.

I'm leaving of my own accord, she'd said, and Otskai could well imagine her stubborn cousin saying such. *If you value my life, you will let me go and find my own way.*

Watkeuse's father had allowed her to go, even though it made him look weak in the eyes of his people. He'd never seemed to understand his daughter or know how to speak in a way that would make her want to obey, but Otskai had never doubted his love for her cousin. A love he showed in his grief over the next several moons.

He'd grieved as if she died, but every so often, Otskai would find him standing at the edge of camp, gazing at the mountains to the east. As if watching for Watkeuse's return.

It shouldn't have surprised her that this was the request he made of the white men. Nor that he would tell them to bring

Otskai along. Her uncle must not have been as blind to his daughter's tendencies as Otskai had always thought.

Now, when they found Watkeuse, would she be willing to go home? Assuming she was alive and well.

A new fear needled through Otskai's chest. Watkeuse *had* to be well. She couldn't let her mind travel that path.

But what if she was married? Would she come back, at least to visit her father and mother? Maybe. But would that be enough for the great chief Runs Bear?

Adam's horse shook its head, bringing Otskai back to the present. The Shoshone. What could she say of them? "There was one woman. About five-and-thirty winters old. Five braves." A new memory pierced. "The woman belonged to a man with a burn on the side of his face." She touched her right cheek. "Like he fell in the fire."

She glanced over at Adam to see if that sounded familiar to him.

His brow was lowered in thought. "A burn? On the right side?" He murmured the words as though they would resurrect a memory.

Then he blinked and turned to her. "Twin Elk? The son of chief Long Hair?"

Twin Elk. The name struck a familiar tone in her mind. "Maybe."

His brow lowered again. "I do remember him having a wife. A friendly woman, but more forward then most."

Otskai pinched back a smile. That would describe the Shoshone woman who'd gained Watkeuse's good opinion so quickly. "That could be the one."

Adam nodded, his expression taking on a distant look. "I'll have to think on where their camp was located. We stopped at several, and I think they were the second group we met."

She hated to quench his budding flame of memory, but recalling their location might not help. "The Shoshone move with the animals. They may not still be in the place they were before winter."

A long breath slipped from Adam. "You're right. We'll have to pray God leads us to them."

Words tumbled out before she could stop them. "You believe in the same God as Caleb?"

Surprise flickered in Adam's eyes, and he nodded. "I do."

"He is leading you on a good path? The one He plans for you?" Her mouth seemed to have taken leave of her good sense, spouting the questions her heart had been dwelling on.

His eyes smiled as he nodded again. "He is. And I look forward to that path one day taking me to heaven. After my time here on earth."

The afterlife. She'd heard the shaman tell of it once, but the ways of reaching it—at least the good afterlife—had never made sense to her.

"How will your God bring you to the life after this one?" She steeled herself for something no sensible mind would believe.

Adam's brows rose. "I am His. He offered to forgive my sins, put behind me all the bad things I've done. I accepted that gift. I live my life following Him. When I die on earth, He will take me to a place he's prepared for me. Heaven."

His gaze deepened on her. "He offers this chance to everyone. He created you. He loves you. He has a good path for you to walk. He wants you to accept His forgiveness, a chance to put the wrong things behind you and follow Him. Then one day, if you choose this, you, too, will join Him in heaven."

He put it so simply, laid out a picture that called to her in its simplicity. In the image Adam painted, she wouldn't have to find her own way in this life.

She worked so hard. And she accomplished much, yet it never seemed enough. There was always more. Always something she failed at, like protecting her son. Could God forgive those failures, put those bad things behind her? Could He show her a better way? She wasn't sure she could stand putting her life under the control of another man who would be scrutinizing her every move. Expecting perfection.

Was that what God would require?

But before she could voice that last question, Caleb's body slumped on the horse in front of her, collapsing on the mare's neck.

CHAPTER 15

Otskai slid a glance at the man issuing ragged breaths beside her. Caleb had been feverish much of the night, which had twisted her stomach into a tight worried knot. She'd awakened often to check on him and wipe his brow with a cold-water cloth. She'd only done so when the heat within made him restless, but finally this morning, he seemed to sleep easier.

She'd known riding all day would be too much for him. If only she'd pushed harder to wait. Most of the claw marks seemed to be healing, but one on his right shoulder and one on his belly had turned a festering pink.

She pressed down the fear that tried to rise in her chest. She'd applied a new poultice of witch hazel leaves a while ago. Since only those two marks were worsening, maybe he would recover yet. The breaking of the fever had to be a good sign.

French had taken her son hunting—not actually hunting he'd assured, more like looking for animals. But River Boy's smile had bloomed wide when they'd sauntered down the valley, the boy perched atop the man's shoulders.

Most of the others were moving in and out of camp as

needed to accomplish what had to be done. Susanna had succumbed to a late morning nap.

Before lying down, she'd given Otskai a treasure. Something she called a needle and thread for sewing—exactly the things used to stitch Caleb's blanket before.

Now, Otskai worked to make the same tight stitches to close the loose flaps on the material. The cloth was still frayed, but it possessed a softness to rival the finest rabbit fur.

Caleb's breathing quieted, a sign he might be waking. At first, his body didn't move, but then one eyelid lifted. It seemed as though that eye was a scout sent to discover the surrounding area, then report back before the rest of him came to life.

When that eye caught sight of her, his entire face seemed to relax. The eyelid closed, and a hint of a smile played at his lips. She'd never seen a man so generous with his smiles. He couldn't know what a gift each one was, easing the tightness inside her every time.

She worked to keep the emotion from her voice. "How are you feeling?"

His eyes stayed shut and his lips seemed to stick as he tried to part them. She should find some bear grease to keep them from paining him.

"Fine. Feeling real fine."

Even in a foreign tongue, she knew a lie when she heard one. But that was Caleb, always seeing things a few shades better than they were.

"Good." She set the blanket she was working on to the side. "I will get bear grease for your lips and bark tea to drink. What else? More stew?"

He gave the tiniest nod of his chin, eyes still closed. "That would be nice." His head must pain him, along with everything else.

Adam's scramble to catch Caleb from falling off the horse

had kept his head from striking the ground, but the tumble couldn't have helped his existing injuries.

She had both liquids keeping warm in the coals, so it didn't take long to retrieve a cup of each, along with the bear grease from Elan's healing kit. Better to save that last item for after he ate, lest everything be tainted with a sour taste. Willow bark would be bitter enough.

She settled beside Caleb. "Stew first."

He opened both eyes partway and positioned his elbows to rise up on them. But at his wince, she touched a hand to his arm. "Just lift your head." She scooted forward so she could slip a hand behind his head while she used the other to lift the cup to his lips.

The intimacy of the position washed through her. He kept his hair shorter than most, and the ends slipped over her fingers, wrapping its fullness around her. Even his head was big, proportionate to the rest of him. In this position, she was nearly hugging him.

The odor of fever that still lingered around him didn't disguise that unique scent that was Caleb's—tender strength, if those attributes could have a smell. She'd always thought those two traits—tenderness and strength—were at odds with each other, but they both fit so perfectly on him.

After three gulps, he eased back from the cup, and his breathing was loud as he worked to draw in air. His eyelids slipped open for a quick glance at her, then closed just as quickly.

At least he had that mercy on her. If he'd held those midnight blue eyes on her very long, she would have ceased breathing completely. As it was, she had to think about every measured intake.

He drank two more sips of broth, then seemed spent.

She eased his head back down to the fur and waited till his

labored breathing slowed. "Can you drink tea now? It will help with pain." Anything he could manage would benefit.

Another single nod of his chin. She slipped her hand behind his head again. He seemed less able to lift himself this time, but working together, he managed four sips of the tea.

When he'd settled once more, she reached for the bear grease. "This goes on your mouth. Make feel better."

As she dabbed a bit on her fingertip and smeared it across his full lower lip, her chest ceased breathing altogether. Awareness of him spiked through every part of her.

His lips were just right for a man. Not too full, not too thin. Just as strong and sturdy as the rest of him, though they'd cracked from the fever. She might have run her finger over them a time or two more than needed.

But even when she'd caressed his mouth as much as she could, she still had a little bear grease left on her finger. The stuff was thick enough to cover a whole arm with only a few drops.

Her gaze slid down to his hands resting atop his fur covering. Winter had dried them, making the knuckles crack as much as his lips had.

She stroked her finger across the knuckles of his right hand, and he shifted to give her better access. They were so dry, she needed another dab of bear grease. She smoothed the ointment over every part of his hand, weaving her fingers between his as she rubbed it into the webs between each one. Maybe he wouldn't think this as intimate as it felt to her.

Yet she couldn't bring herself to stop, and the dryness of his skin gave her reason to continue. When that hand had absorbed everything it would, she reached for his other one, pulling it closer so she could massage the grease over every part.

At last, she could find no more excuse to continue and gave the back of his hand a final stroke with her thumb. Then she pulled back, rubbing her hands together to soak in the last of the grease. But in truth, she wanted to soak in the warmth of his touch. The feel of him, both rough and strong, and so capable, even in this vulnerable state.

She dropped her hands to her lap and let herself watch him for a moment. She probably shouldn't allow herself the luxury of staring so openly. Maybe she should take up her work on the blanket again, but she didn't want to smudge the cloth with grease marks.

Perhaps Caleb was so weary he'd already begun to doze and wouldn't realize she was watching him. Besides, considering the thorough massage she'd just given his hands, studying him seemed far more innocent.

His eyes never opened, but he shifted his hand from the fur to lay on the ground in front of her, palm up. He flattened his fingers, as though he wanted her to lay something there.

Then an awareness sank through her. He wanted her hand.

Did she dare? Every intimate touch between them so far had had a reason. Even the other day by the creek when he'd brushed her cheek to wipe away tears. Even when he'd held her hand by the water for solace. Even the thorough caress of his hands that she'd just performed with the bear grease.

But if she were to place her hand in his now, it would break the barrier of mere friendship. She would be pulling the blanket off her heart and acknowledging her attraction for him. He *had* become more to her than merely a friend—a friend who did far more to help her than he should.

Did she dare?

Good sense told her to rise and run far away. But maybe her actions moments before had stolen too much of her control. She *wanted* to place her hand in his. Wanted to acknowledge the way she felt about him, at least in part.

So…she reached out and covered his palm with her own.

CALEB WAS GETTING STRONGER. And it wasn't the stew and willow bark Otskai and Elan kept plying him with that was helping so much.

No. His turning point had been that moment when Otskai placed her hand in his—that slight revealing of her heart. Finally.

Inside, he'd been whooping and spinning her in circles, though outwardly, he'd only managed what might have barely passed for a smile.

But as the rest of that day had passed, he ate stew and drank tea until his body could hold no more liquid. The trip to find a secluded tree had helped too, even if he was leaning on Beaver Tail for the walking. At least he'd gotten up and moved around.

And when Otskai had presented him with the quilt she'd repaired, the moment had filled him with enough pleasure to keep him going for days. The blanket had been a parting gift from the Reverend and Mrs. Sandifer when he'd left to take his position as minister in his own church.

Being a reverend himself had been an awful debacle, but he still treasured those two people who had poured so much good into his life. He would be far less of a man today without their guidance. And he'd treasured that quilt, keeping it close by for the times loneliness crept over him. He'd not minded the stitches coming loose, except that he hadn't wanted to lose any part of this treasure.

But Otskai had repaired the broken parts. She may never know how much that single act meant to him. Now, the quilt would last longer than it would have, and she'd become part of its specialness too.

The women insisted they stay in camp another day, and he tried to use the time to help as much as he could. Mostly telling the boy stories and playing games with rocks. He had a quick mind, this son of Otskai. Quicker already than some grown men.

But this was the last day he would let them delay on his account. Come tomorrow morning, he'd have to put his foot down. His good foot, at least.

They needed to set out on the trail, and he'd be fine. The burning in the cuts on his shoulders and belly had finally eased, so he really *would* be fine.

Now though, River Boy had finally dozed off under the cloudy night sky with his head snuggled next to Caleb's, just the way he usually did with his mama. Maybe he needed that reassuring touch, even in sleep.

Caleb had watched them sleep this way so many times, the boy's cute little face snugged next to her beautiful one. And even while he admired the view, he wondered how in the world she could sleep with someone pressed so close to her.

Now he knew.

With the lad's temple hugging his cheek, the boy's arm laid across Caleb's shoulder, the urge grew strong to cradle him even closer, to protect him from anything that might bring pain —either to body or heart. He'd be content to lie like this all night.

One of the forms moving around the campfire stepped away from the light and stepped closer to him. Otskai crept to his side and eased down to her knees.

She reached to take the boy, but Caleb raised a staying hand. "He can sleep here." He kept his voice low, but the rumble of his baritone might still wake the lad. He rested his hand on River Boy's small shoulder.

The firelight shone on one side of Otskai's face, casting the other side in deep shadows. Yet he could see enough in that one eye to catch a glimmer of uncertainty.

"Truly, he's welcome here. Lay your blankets nearby if you want to stay close." He motioned to an empty spot near enough the fire where she should stay warm, and not too close to his pallet to be unseemly.

He hoped.

In truth, even riding beside her in the saddle all day seemed intimate, yet not nearly close enough. His heart had latched hold of this woman in a way he'd never thought possible.

Lord, let her continue to open to me. Please.

CHAPTER 16

Three more days in the saddle, and Caleb had learned to lock his jaw and bear the pain.

In truth, the gashes across his upper body had dulled to little more than a persistent ache. And the swelling in most of them had settled. Several of the claw marks were deep enough they could have been stitched at the time of the attack. But it had likely been too dark to realize it that night. Either way, he'd carry the scars for the rest of his life. A reminder of a journey that would change him forever. Hopefully in a good way, but that remained to be seen.

He adjusted the position of his injured foot, which he'd taken to propping on his mare's neck as he rode. Good thing Bessie was a sturdy girl. They'd secured a stick next to his ankle with wrapping to keep the bone straight when he wasn't sitting beside a creek to soak the joint.

Bessie's ears perked at the same moment a whistle sounded from Beaver Tail in the lead of their group. Caleb jerked his gaze ahead to see what they spotted. Maybe fifty strides beyond them, a rider was coming around the side of the mountain.

An Indian, from the feathers tied in his black hair.

Another man appeared behind him, then two more rode around the curve of the slope. Caleb strained to spot any identifying marks on the men or horses. The animals weren't painted, as far as he could tell. So hopefully not a war party. Nor did the horses have spots like those owned by the Nimiipuu.

Could these be Shoshone? A handful of other tribes lived in these parts—Crow, Flathead, and a few more. These could even be Blackfoot come down from the north.

He shot a glance toward Beaver Tail and Susanna, who rode just ahead of Caleb. He couldn't see BT's face, and his posture gave no hint of whether he considered the oncomers friend or foe. If only Caleb knew enough about this land and its people to know for himself.

He sent a glance back at Otskai, whose attention was also honed on the strangers.

"Who are they?" He kept his voice low enough that it wouldn't carry past her.

River Boy squirmed in her arms, and she fired a sharp command to him that Caleb couldn't decipher. That no-nonsense tone accomplished its goal, and the lad stilled, uncertainty shadowing his eyes.

Otskai returned her focus to the strangers as she answered Caleb's question. *"Tiiwelka."* She shook her head as if clearing the thought. "Shoshone."

Both her voice and her posture held a tense edge. Not a bit of excitement at finding her cousin or at least people who could point them in the right direction.

The Shoshone and Nimiipuu hadn't always been at peace. In truth, from what he'd seen of the few interactions with Shoshone on their journey west, the truce between the tribes was very unsteady, with little trust on either side. Maybe that was what caused her angst now—a distrust instilled by her kinfolk.

He shifted his focus back to the oncoming men, who were now half the distance ahead of them.

Beaver raised a hand to signal a halt, and Caleb reined his mare in along with the rest of them.

Beaver Tail never glanced back as he called, "Adam."

The man must have been ready for the summons, for he was trotting his mount past Caleb only a second after BT called him.

Adam and Otskai were the only ones who had met the Shoshone group Watkeuse left with. Good thing Beaver didn't invite Otskai forward into that vulnerable position, especially with her son perched in front of her. If he had, Caleb would have ridden up with them. Or maybe even tried to coax Otskai to stay back a little. She might not have listened, but he would have found a way to keep her and the lad safe.

In tandem, Adam and Beaver Tail rode ahead, and after a few seconds, two of the Shoshone split off from the others to meet them in the middle. That they were willing to meet for a peace talk was a good sign these fellows didn't intend to fight.

Lord, let them know of Watkeuse. Use them to lead us to her.

As they waited, Otskai eased her horse up alongside his, then farther forward beside Susanna, who now sat in the lead. Otskai probably wanted a better look at the men, but he didn't like having the women and child up there on the front line of defense, no matter how capable they were.

He nudged his mare up beside Otskai. They couldn't hear anything the men ahead were saying, so he ventured a quiet question. "Do you know them?"

For a long moment, she didn't answer. Thankfully, River Boy sat contentedly in her lap, part of a fist in his mouth and his focus on the men ahead.

At last, Otskai tipped her head. "I don't know." Another pause. "Maybe."

Hope tried to spring in his chest, both nurtured and squashed by her vague answer. He'd have to wait and see.

Then she spoke again. "I think I've seen the one in front of Adam. But I don't recall when."

That made more sense. She'd probably seen a number of Shoshone in her lifetime, so recalling exactly when she saw one particular man couldn't be easy.

Finally, the two pairs of men in the center separated, Adam and Beaver riding back toward their group. As usual, BT's face was impossible to read. Not even a hint of whether these men had helped or not.

Adam's expression usually showed emotion far easier, but his look now seemed almost perplexed. No sign of pleasure or relief. But at least he didn't appear disappointed.

When the two reached them and halted, Adam spoke first. "They've seen the band led by Twin Elk. The one Watkeuse left with. He saw them in the winter when snow was thickest, and he gave us directions to the place. They spoke of finding buffalo herds when the snow melted, so we need to hurry. And pray they haven't left that place yet."

An urgency pressed in Caleb's spirit. *Lord. So close. Make them stay put. Help us catch them.*

Within moments, the four Shoshone braves had moved down the mountain and disappeared behind a group of boulders.

Their group pushed onward, following the path the Shoshone had come, but in the opposite direction. Adam and Beaver Tail led, with Susanna and Otskai just behind.

The trail allowed two side-by-side, so Meksem pulled alongside Caleb. She led Adam's new horse, Tesoro. The one she'd traded the tomahawk for as a gift for Adam.

Meksem always seemed quiet, reserved. So it was hard to get to know her. But that act of selflessness in giving her prized possession as a gift for Adam was enough to make Caleb like the woman.

He sent her a smile now, or at least as much of a grin as he could muster through the throbbing in his head and leg. After so many days of this pain, he was turning a bit grumpy. He worked not to let it show, though.

Her eyes smiled back at him and seemed to read through the pleasant façade he was fighting to keep. "You hide your pain well. I know it must be strong."

She likely did know. Meksem didn't waste her breath with idle words. And she was well trained as a warrior, which meant she'd experienced her share of wounds.

But no need to belabor the point by focusing on his pain. This time his smile felt stronger. "I wouldn't want to foist a grumpy man on you all."

A glimmer lit her gaze. "You're a good leader, Caleb Jackson."

The words struck him like a needle piercing skin. He wasn't a good leader. The church he'd tried to pastor back in Indiana had wholeheartedly decided that. He might be good with people he knew. Those he didn't have to worry about judging him. But standing in front of a crowd, attempting to guide their spiritual growth...he'd been a complete failure.

He might've volunteered to leave that church, but they'd eagerly packed his bags and waved farewell.

Meksem's words turned over in his mind again. *You're a good leader.* Not *I'll bet you would be.* She spoke as if he was *now* leading.

Not this group. He was good at coming alongside, encouraging. Just call him Barnabas from the Bible. He was no Paul. Not the one planning and guiding the expedition.

O*tskai carried* a plate of food toward the water where Caleb sat soaking his ankle. She motioned her son forward. "Come. Find Caleb."

River Boy toddled in a meandering path beside her, but

those words gave him purpose. They were the same ones Caleb used during games of hide-and-go-seek. The big man would tuck himself behind a tree or boulder and call, *Find Caleb.*

River Boy would totter toward the voice, giggling all the way. When he found the man, the giggles would turn to belly laughs as the two wrestled in a tickling match. The sound of the two voices laughing hysterically, one high and one deep, made a beautiful chorus that lightened her chest every time.

They hadn't played that game since Caleb's tangle with the bear, but her son hadn't forgotten the words.

He stepped forward now with purpose, lifting his little feet to clear the grass as he toddled forward.

The man had turned a grin on them, anticipation gleaming in his gaze as he watched the lad's approach. His gaze flicked up to her once, loosing a flutter in her chest as he smiled. His grins had been much tenser these past days, probably from the pain he suffered through without complaint.

As River Boy neared him, the boy's little feet raced. Then a foot snagged in the grass, catapulting him forward. Caleb scooped him up, lifting him high, even from his sitting position. Then he laid him across his lap and set in to tickle.

Her son giggled and snorted and laughed until he couldn't breathe.

Otskai soaked in the sight of her boy so happy, of this man making him so. She dropped to her knees beside them, still holding the plate. Watching their antics.

At last, the two came up for air. Both breathing hard, smiles splitting their faces and sparkling their eyes.

Caleb gazed her way, and for a heartbeat, he looked as though he might lean forward and brush a kiss to her mouth.

Her heart raced, her chest fluttering. Part of her wanted that, but part of her jerked back inside herself.

He must've seen that flinch, for his smile eased. Some of the joy left his eyes, and he shifted his attention to the boy, settling the lad on his good leg.

Then he glanced at the plate in her hands. "That for me?" His words were light, easy going.

No hint of disappointment. Nothing that should make her feel uncomfortable.

But a sadness rose inside her. He would do whatever he could to make those around him happy, especially her and her son. Caleb was such a good man. If she could trust herself with anyone, it was him.

But did she dare risk her freedom?

She handed over the plate, and he nestled it in the grass beside him. They'd not cooked fresh food but had heated smoked salmon and baked camas root, so at least the meal was warm.

As Caleb picked up a chunk of camas, her son opened his mouth and grunted, the sign he wanted a bite.

A smile touched Caleb's eyes as he held the food up to River Boy's mouth. After the boy bit down, Caleb took his own bite. Contentment eased over both their faces as they chewed.

Still, Caleb deserved to eat all she'd brought him. She held out her hands. "I'll take him to the fire to feed him."

The lad opened his mouth for another bite like a baby bird waiting for a worm.

Caleb shook his head as he accommodated, letting River Boy bite off a piece his size. "He's fine here." He sent her a contented look. "He's good company." Then a new thought seemed to register and his brows rose. "Unless you need him?"

She shook her head. In truth, she'd had the keeping of the boy all day, both in her saddle and when they'd stopped. She was more than willing for a few moments to accomplish what she needed without half her mind and focus split to keep up with the lad.

A twinge pricked her chest. How could she one moment

long to cradle her son and never let him go and the next long for just a few minutes alone, without responsibility for him? No matter how much she tried to be a good mother, she failed. Even in this.

Perhaps Caleb heard her thoughts—hopefully not—but he said, "Go, do what you need to, Otskai. He's safe with me." As if to reinforce his words, he tightened his hand around her son and gave the leg River Boy sat on a little bounce. The lad beamed a mouthful of food at her.

Another smile slipped through Otskai's chest. She pressed up to standing, then backed away. "I'll bring my food to eat here too." And she would bring enough for her little bird also.

The others already sat eating by the fire, so she quickly filled a plate and found a cup to dip from the clear stream. She set water to boil with a few leaves of boneset as a tea for Caleb. She'd not even glanced at his foot to see if the swelling had worsened. She'd have to do that when she returned to them.

When she settled beside Caleb again, he was once again feeding her son a bite. "Look, there's your mama come back." And the look in Caleb's eyes made her think he was also glad she returned. Maybe only for the extra food, but his eyes never glanced at her plate.

"Ma–ma." River Boy's little voice snatched her focus, and it took a moment for the meaning of his sounds to come clear.

A thrill slipped through her. "Mama?" That was the English word for *pike*. He'd never called her such, and she hadn't thought to teach him. She tried not to let the fullness of her pleasure show. Such a little thing shouldn't mean so much.

She moved some of the food from her plate to Caleb's to replace what her son had eaten, then held out a piece of salmon small enough for the boy to chew.

The lad took it but sent a glance to Caleb that held a tiny bit of disappointment. As if he'd hoped to have the specialness of Caleb's attention on him completely. *I know what you mean, son.*

Otskai turned her focus to the water as she bit into her meat. This stream flowed gently. Not a foaming current to be seen. She could sit beside this brook without fear hammering in her chest.

Her gaze slipped to Caleb's foot, and a gasp caught in her throat. She leaned forward to make sure the water wasn't deceiving her eyes, doubling the size of his ankle.

Nay, the joint had swollen and turned a hideous dark color.

"Caleb." She set her plate aside and moved to her knees at the edge of the water, then reached in and gingerly touched his bruised skin. The creek ran icy, and his flesh felt tight and almost springy. Just that single touch sent a sluice of pain through her that must be nothing compared to his own agony.

She looked back at him to see his reaction. Now the shadows under his eyes made sense. The lines at the corners that weren't the right angle to be from a smile. She'd let herself focus so much on her own trials through each day that she'd convinced herself his had lessened only because he didn't speak of them.

"What can I do to make it better?" She searched his face, then turned back to the foot to study it. The tea brewing would help lessen the swelling, and she could add willow bark to help with his pain. What more could be done? The cold water would help best of all. She would tell the others how bad his leg had become and make sure they stayed in this place at least another day.

She pushed to her feet and turned back toward camp. She would do these things before another moment of his pain passed by.

CHAPTER 17

By the time the tea had steeped enough for Otskai to scoop out the first cup full, Caleb and her son had finished eating. River Boy knelt at the edge of the water, splashing in the cold liquid. Somehow, Caleb had managed to keep him from running into the stream completely, although she'd have to change the boy into a new tunic when he finished.

She knelt beside Caleb and held out the tea.

"Thank you." As he reached for the cup, his gaze spoke the same message, and its intensity pressed warmth deep in her chest.

A burn crept up her throat, stinging her nose. How could he think of her when he was in so much pain? So much he'd done for her on this journey, and even before, with saving her son and building the fence. Yet she'd let herself stay ignorant of his agony, turning a blind eye to a need so obvious.

Maybe she shouldn't put the responsibility fully on her shoulders. He could've asked for help. Spoken of his pain. She shouldn't let her emotions run so freely. But as her gaze wandered to his hideous limb, the burn crept up to her eyes. If there was anything she could do to make this better for him, she would.

"It's all right." Caleb's soft rumble pulled her back to him. His eyes were soft, a warm blanket. "The ankle's getting better. I know it doesn't look like it, but the leg doesn't hurt nearly as bad."

He couldn't be speaking the truth, not with the size of the swelling.

But he motioned to the plate she'd left unattended. "Sit and eat."

She sent a glance toward her son, who'd stood and was toddling back toward the group by the campfire.

Susanna rose and moved toward them, holding her hand out to River Boy. She directed her words toward Otskai. "We'll go for a walk to stretch our legs."

Otskai nodded her consent. Hopefully a little of her gratitude showed as well.

When the two left, walking toward where the horses were hobbled to graze, Otskai picked up her plate. She'd been hungry before, but the food no longer held appeal.

"Eat." Caleb's voice nudged her attention toward him. A corner of his mouth curved. "Shall I feed you like I did the lad?"

His voice teased, but then he actually reached for the camas root and lifted it to her mouth. He didn't hold the food so close she couldn't refuse, but near enough she could lean forward and bite. He held the base of the root, so her mouth wasn't in danger of touching his hand. But still, the intimacy of him feeding her…

She took in a breath for courage and leaned forward, closing her teeth around the edge of the root. The camas held more flavor than she'd expected, but the intense sweetness came more from his nearness than anything the food possessed.

She didn't dare look at his face as she chewed, keeping her mouth as dainty as she could manage. How did the white women he was accustomed to eat? She'd only seen Susanna and had never noticed much difference in her manner of chewing. She should have paid closer attention.

Caleb still held the root up, waiting for her to take a second bite, it seemed. She couldn't stop herself from looking up to his face this time. She had to know what thoughts played across his eyes.

She slid a glance to him with no idea of what she might find. And she couldn't quite decipher what expression his strong features wore. Earnestness. Intensity. Something more she would fall into if she let herself linger there.

So she returned her focus to the camas root and bit again. His hand never wavered, even with the pressure of her teeth biting into the food. This man possessed strength well beyond her own, and not just physical ability. When she finished chewing the second portion, she gathered more courage to check his expression again.

This time the hunger in his eyes was impossible to miss. He yearned for her as she did him. A sensation of strength slipped through her. She leaned in the smallest bit. He read the motion, and the yearning in his gaze intensified.

She dropped her focus to his lips, those lips she'd touched only days before when she'd soothed them with bear grease.

He read her meaning well and closed the space between them.

His mouth was gentle, yet not tentative. He possessed too much steadiness for that. Solid, yet tender.

A response rose up within her, but she restrained it at first. How could she be kissing him?

But his touch crept through her, awakening sensations she'd not felt in...had she ever felt them? As she came to life, she raised her hand to cup his cheek. The brush of beard tickled her palm, but its coarseness soothed her. His mouth treasured hers, giving only. Not taking. Infusing her with strength and confidence.

When he pulled back, her breaths came harder. But a lightness lifted inside her.

His hand had cradled her neck, fingers brushing the base of her hair. His eyes studied her, a rich blue like the end of a sunset. His gaze caressed her face, much as his lips had done her mouth a moment before.

She wouldn't have thought she could look at him with so much boldness. But there was no longer a barrier between them. The kiss had swept it all away.

"Otskai." He spoke her name with reverence that washed through her, tightening her chest with emotion she wasn't ready to face. What was it about this man that spoke to her heart?

His steadiness. That word didn't capture the essence of him, but it was the closest she could find. Her spirit longed for what he gave her. When he was around, she felt…at home.

A sensation she'd not experienced in so many years.

For long moments, she held his gaze. Letting herself stay there, in that warm dwelling place.

But a sound in the distance called her out. Broke through her lingerings.

Caleb's gaze slipped toward the camp. Then with a jolt, her own awareness pressed in. Were the others watching?

She pulled her hand from where it had slipped to his shoulder. His thick, strong shoulder. She scanned the figures around the fire. No one was looking their way. The noise must have been a clang as Elan loaded pots into the food pack.

Easing out a breath, she turned back to meet Caleb's gaze again. This time a bit of shyness crept in.

She'd kissed this man. What now? Did she even want what should usually come next?

She'd not wanted another man. Had confirmed that within herself so many times since Motsqueh's death. Even in the hard nights after River Boy's birth, the times when she'd longed for someone to help with her burdens, she'd only had to remember what it was like to live under a man's sovereign authority, and she'd quickly returned to her senses.

But she couldn't imagine Caleb as that overbearing husband. One who required perfection in everything she did.

She *could* imagine being with him, side-by-side as partners. She could imagine walking alongside him as he carried her son on his shoulders. Bringing joy to them both.

"Will you sit and talk with me?" Caleb reached for her hand and gave a gentle squeeze.

The idea called, but she needed to escape. Needed time to form a picture of what she wanted. The image she'd clung to for so long now seemed tilted. Did she still want freedom? Or could there be something different…something better?

She returned his squeeze, but then pulled back. "I should go help." She shifted to her knees and sent a quick glance to his face, trying for a smile, hoping the expression put him at ease. He might think by her actions that the kiss had frightened her. That would matter to Caleb.

But she couldn't stay here, not with the churning that grew in her chest with every breath.

She pushed up to her feet and fled.

CALEB EASED out a breath as he watched Otskai flee along the creek's bank. His insides still quivered from that kiss, both the power of it and the fact that he'd done what he said he wouldn't. He'd promised himself he wouldn't press her further than she was ready to go.

Yet, that look in her eyes, the way her gaze had dropped to his mouth. He'd thought she wanted the kiss. Everything inside him screamed *yes*.

And she'd responded. He could still feel the strength of her lips as they answered his.

But then she'd come to her senses. Maybe he should have kept kissing her forever, kept them both in that place of connection.

Yet he'd wanted to see her face. To see that she felt for him even a small bit of what burned inside him for her. But the moment he pulled back, he'd seen the shift in her eyes. The awareness. The churning of her mind. She wasn't a woman who gave control easily.

He didn't *want* control of her, but maybe he hadn't done a good job showing that.

She'd not gone to camp to help but had fled upstream, disappearing around a clump of rocks. Which meant she needed time alone.

Help her judge wisely, Lord. Show her Your truth. Show me. Don't let me run ahead of Your will.

SMOKE ROSE IN THE DISTANCE, sending a shiver of apprehension through Caleb's body. Would it be too much to hope whoever camped ahead was a Shoshone band—the specific Shoshone band they sought? Surely, they couldn't be so lucky as to find Watkeuse's group in the first camp they met on the eastern side of the mountains.

The day after the kiss, Otskai had insisted they stay in camp to let Caleb's ankle time to rest. She herself hadn't spent much time in the camp, taking River Boy for hikes along the mountainside during much of the morning and afternoon.

Much as he'd hated to hold the group up, the rest had helped his ankle a great deal. After two more days in the saddle, though, no matter how he tried to keep the leg propped on his mare's neck, the limb had swollen again. A throb pulsed all the way up to his head.

It didn't help that they'd not been able to find a water source the night before. If they could only locate Watkeuse, surely they would stay put for a few days. Long enough that he could get the throbbing under control.

Otskai, Meksem, Adam, and Beaver Tail had clustered at the front of their group, probably discussing how to approach the camp that must be on the other side of the trees and boulders ahead of them.

Maybe Caleb should be involved in the discussion, but the pounding in his head made thinking a challenge. He trusted the others. Among them, they knew this land and its people far better than he did.

As their group neared the trees, the path narrowed and Otskai and Adam dropped back behind Beaver Tail and Meksem. A bit of relief slipped through him that Otskai wasn't on the front line should an arrow come flying. Not that he wanted BT or Meksem in danger, but they were both well-trained warriors. Either could hear the whisper of a mountain lion at fifty paces, he had no doubt.

As they followed a worn trail around a cluster of trees, a lodge appeared in the distance. A few strides later, that one lodge had spread to three, and Indian braves stepped onto the trail. More figures slipped in from the trees on both sides of the path, forming a group of ten or more. None rode horses, but they all wore weapons—hatchets or knives hanging from their waists, and some had bows strapped around their chests.

Beaver Tail didn't slow their group, just kept riding forward as though no strangers weighed heavy with deadly tools approached them.

Caleb had been keeping his own gun in its scabbard, out of the way of his propped leg, instead of resting the rifle across his lap like many of the others. Drawing the weapon now wouldn't be a sign of peace, so he settled for keeping his hand near the stock in case he had to pull the gun quickly.

Let them be peaceful, Lord. When they reached twenty paces apart, Beaver Tail signaled their group to halt. He and Meksem rode forward to parlay.

The Indians ahead didn't send two men to meet them. Instead, all eleven approached. They were near enough now Caleb could count the exact number.

Apprehension churned in his belly, intensifying the mallet whacking his skull as Beaver Tail and Meksem halted to converse with the strangers.

No one appeared angry. A couple of the men held hatchets at their sides, but no new weapons were being drawn. Beaver was probably explaining their purpose in coming. Asking questions.

Though the man came from the Blackfoot tribe, regarded by these people with a bit of fear and no shortage of distrust, Beaver Tail himself was steady, loyal, and as goodhearted as a fellow could be. Anyone who spoke with him more than a few minutes quickly got past the stern exterior to realize those traits.

After a few minutes, a man from the other group motioned to his left as though giving directions. Caleb's heart picked up pace as hope tried to rise within him.

At last, Beaver Tail and Meksem turned and rode back to them. When they reached their group, Beaver Tail gave a quick nod in the direction the man had pointed.

He and Meksem turned their animals that way, and the rest of them fell into step behind. Riding two abreast as they were, Susanna rode beside Caleb, with Otskai in front of him. Even with the nagging pain pulsing through him, his gaze didn't miss the slim curve of Otskai's form. River Boy rode with Elan near the back of the group, so Otskai sat alone, tall and poised. At one with the mount beneath her. A woman who took his breath away.

A few minutes after they'd ridden out of sight of the braves, the confident outline of Otskai's form stiffened. His sluggish mind took an extra heartbeat to seek out the reason why. Then a rustling sound drifted on the wind.

A river.

They'd been blessed that, after her tumultuous swim, all the water they'd crossed had been fairly shallow. He'd told himself after she'd panicked at their first crossing that he wouldn't let her cross alone if they met another river deep enough to require the horses to swim. He had to help her this time, but would he be capable with his broken leg?

From the rushing sounds ahead, the coming river moved fast with a high swell of water. As loud as the noise was growing, there might even be a waterfall.

Lord, it'd be awfully nice if we didn't have to cross that. Couldn't we just ride alongside it for a while?

No peace pressed into his soul. No reassurance they wouldn't need to face the rushing current.

And that started a churning in his middle. How would Otskai handle this crossing?

CHAPTER 18

The water came into view, and the wide expanse of surging current didn't help the bile in Caleb's belly. Even if the horses didn't have to swim, this would be a challenge for Otskai.

What of her son? He glanced back at Elan and the boy, riding two horses behind him.

She held the lad tight, her shoulders back, chin raised in confident determination. She met Caleb's gaze with a firm nod. Her hand inched a little tighter around the lad, making it clear she would let nothing happen to him.

Elan had grown up in this land, fording these rivers. Of course, Otskai had too, but he had a feeling some event in her past had planted this fear in her.

He'd crossed dozens of rivers alongside Elan, and she'd never once blinked at a swift current, even when the horses struggled to swim. Also, Adam rode by her side and could help, should the crossing prove treacherous.

That left Otskai for him to focus on, and he swung his attention back to her. They were a dozen strides from the water now, and her entire body seemed made of iron—the kind that didn't bend. Inflexible, locked into whatever shape the blacksmith melded it into.

Using his hand to help, he lowered his injured leg from its resting position on his mare's neck until it hung at the horse's side. He may not be able to use the lower part of that limb, but he'd need the rest of his body secure in the saddle for whatever would be required of him.

A hundred strides upriver, a waterfall cascaded over a ledge. That contributed to the noise, but the section in front of them flowed swiftly, spinning around rocks and foaming as it dipped over boulders beneath the surface.

His eyes traced out a way across the river that looked unencumbered by rocks. At least, those he could see on the surface. But had the Indians offered any insight about where to cross? He needed to know Beaver Tail's plan.

He nudged Bessie up to the front of the group. As he passed Otskai, her gaze was locked on the water. Better he learn the plan before trying to assure her. When he reined his mare beside Beaver Tail, he had to raise his voice above the water, now only five strides in front of them. "Where do we plan to cross?"

Beaver Tail raised an arm to point to the route Caleb had spotted before, then lifted his finger to point to peaks rising on the other side of the river. "They said there's a Nimiipuu woman living in the Shoshone camp between those two mountains. They didn't know her name."

The two mountains he motioned to were directly opposite them, so it made sense to cross the water here. A glance in both directions showed no better place. The bank was barren of brush, covered with trampled grass, as though herds sometimes came to drink or cross. Buffalo maybe, or perhaps deer or elk.

That meant this was likely the best fording place around. He would just have to make sure Otskai made it across safely.

When they halted their horses in at the water's edge, he maneuvered Bessie beside Otskai. She was gripping her saddle with both sets of white knuckles, her gaze locked on a spot in the middle of the river where the water foamed around a cluster of boulders. Her shoulders didn't move, but her chest eased out and in with steady, although very light, breaths. Her brown skin had paled lighter than his own.

"Otskai." He kept his voice low so he wouldn't draw the others' attention. It only took a glance, though, to see that the rest of the group had noticed and were waiting patiently for how they could help. Lord willing, the crossing wouldn't be hard, so he and Otskai would be able to manage together.

His quiet voice didn't seem to penetrate her terror, so he tried a little louder. "Otskai."

Her head shifted, but she didn't focus on him. Apparently, his voice was not enough to draw her away from the water holding her transfixed.

He laid a hand on her sleeve.

She jerked her gaze to his, her eyes wide and a bit feral. He closed his hand around her arm, his grip not tight but solid enough to hold her steady.

"Ride with me." He nodded toward the back of his saddle. "Behind me."

Her gaze flicked there, then back to his face. Her actions were so quick, the terror on her face so real, it seemed she wasn't thinking straight. And they hadn't even set foot in the water yet.

He nudged Bessie closer. "Climb on behind me." When he tugged on her arm, she finally lifted her leg to slide behind the back of his saddle. It would be a tight fit between him and his bedroll, but being held snug might make her feel more secure.

Moving her from one horse to the other was more awkward then he'd expected. Otskai's thoughts seemed to be moving slowly—her reactions sluggish—but at least she was breathing more freely once she was settled behind him.

Meksem took the reins of Otskai's mare since she didn't have a packhorse to lead like some of the others did. Good thing Caleb didn't have his hands full with a horse tethered behind him either.

Otskai sat stiff at his back. Surely she'd ridden double before. Her people were famous for the horses they raised, and she'd proved her savvy with her own mount. The water must still be holding her frozen.

He patted his side. "Wrap your arms around me to hold on."

She did so, placing tentative hands on either side of his belly. Not quite a wrap, but he laid his arm to cover both her hands and hold them secure. Surely she'd cling tight when they were in the water.

When he gave Beaver the *all clear* nod, the man nudged his horse into the water. Bessie eased in behind Susanna's mount, with Meksem riding up behind them.

The moment his mare's front hoof struck the water, Otskai's hold clamped tight around him. She didn't move her hands closer to the center of his belly so they would be more secure, just squeezed his sides in a vise.

He kept his body relaxed, trying to send that confidence through her. She didn't seem to be soaking it in though. With Bessie's second step, the sound of Otskai's breathing ceased.

He rubbed a fingertip across the back of her wrist as the mare continued into the water. The surface came up above the animal's knees now, and ahead of them the swirling river had nearly reached the neck on Beaver Tail's mount. The animals would be swimming soon, and the current was already pressing them sideways as they fought to move forward.

The sound of Otskai's breathing finally whispered in his ear, barely rising above the rushing water. Her breaths were back to those measured, shallow intakes. She'd be blue by the time they reached the other bank.

Bessie plodded forward, and a wave licked Caleb's toe, soaking part of his moccasin. Otskai wasn't wet yet, but she would be soon. He'd better settle her now before things got worse.

Leaning back to let her feel his nearness, he took her hands and worked them toward the middle of his belly. Though her palms were flat against him, she pressed hard enough he had to pry them up to move her grip. "You'll have a better hold if you wrap all the way around me." He turned his head so she could hear his words, and another slip of a breath brushed his cheek.

His chest ached at the root of her fear, whatever had planted this terror inside her. *Lord, show me how to make this better for her.*

He turned a little more toward her, the better to see her face. Her arms tightened around him, a more secure hold this time. He only managed a glance at her eyes, those beautiful dark orbs that always connected with him. "You're safe, Otskai. I'll keep you safe. God will bring us across without harm." *Please, Lord. Let those words hold true.*

If she answered, he didn't hear it over the rush of the water. But her breath fanned his face, a deeper exhale than before.

A glance farther back showed Elan moving steadily with River Boy in her hold. Both seemed composed, and the lad wore a wide smile. Of course.

Better Caleb keep his focus on Otskai. Turning forward again, he planted his arm over her hands, giving her wrist another caress.

Just in time, too, for Bessie stepped into a low spot, plunging their legs into the wet. The mare's feet scrambled for purchase, and after a few faulty steps, she began to swim.

He leaned forward to help the horse as much as he could. Otskai squeezed his waist hard enough to push out some organs, and he closed his hand around her wrist, just in case something happened and she lost hold of him.

He *wouldn't* lose hold of her.

Good thing Bessie had always been a strong swimmer, for the weight of two riders would have pushed a lesser mare under as she fought the swift current. They'd almost cleared the middle of the river. Ahead of them, Susanna's horse was finding solid footing again.

Just a little farther.

We're almost there, girl. He might've been talking to the horse or the woman gasping behind him. Of the two, Bessie seemed the more collected, swimming with intentional strokes.

But then she hit something—a rock probably. She went down, all but her nostrils plunging below the water.

Otskai screamed, and Caleb gripped her wrist tighter as he pushed them away from the horse. Bessie needed all her strength and balance to fight against the current. He'd have to get Otskai to safety himself.

With a hard tug, he pulled her around to his side, wrapping one arm around her and plunging the other into the water for a hard stroke.

With his first kick, pain sliced up his injured leg. He bit back a howl.

The current pressed hard, sending them both a face full of water. He fought to use his free arm and good leg to push forward. After three strokes, his foot struck ground.

A rock too slippery to stand on, but his next try found a groove between two stones. He pulled Otskai up with him, but with only one strong foot, he wasn't able to stand. Pushing against the current, he strained toward the bank.

Beaver Tail had seen their debacle and was riding back toward them. Susanna aimed her mount toward Bessie, who'd been dragged downstream by the current before she'd finally found solid footing. If Caleb had the energy and breath, he would tell her not to worry. Once Bessie reached dry land, she'd shake off, then find grass and wait for him.

But he only had the strength to focus on Otskai.

Unlike the last time he'd dragged her from a rushing river, she was walking now. They clung together. Keeping each other upright, her shivering and him barely able to put weight on his injured ankle.

Beaver reached them and spun his horse to face the direction they were going. Caleb repositioned Otskai under his arm to give her more freedom to walk but still held her enough to keep her from falling. Then he grabbed Beaver's saddle with his other hand to use as a crutch.

Three abreast, they trudged over the river rock until they reached the bank. When they stepped onto dry ground, Otskai sank from his hold, slipping to the grass as though all her strength had fled. He dropped to his knees beside her, sucking in breath to start his lungs working again.

"Are you hurt?" He pressed his hands to his thighs and drew in another inhale.

She shook her head, fighting for breath as much as he was. Her face held more color than before, which seemed like a good sign.

This time had been better than the other crossing. She'd kept enough presence of mind to walk out at the end. But he couldn't shake the image of her before they'd begun. Staring out at the overflowing river, her face had blanched and her lungs were barely sipping faint breaths. Yet even those tiny inhales were measured, as though she counted out each one.

Whatever had happened to her in the past had nearly crippled this woman who was so strong in every other situation. Every part of him wanted to know that story. Had the event been recent? Or when she was a little girl, helpless and innocent?

He'd thought to let her have her privacy. Allow her to one

day open up when she was ready. But before they crossed another river, he needed to know about the event that had scarred her.

Tonight, when she was dry and recovered, he would ask. And pray she trusted him with what must be her deepest fear.

CHAPTER 19

This felt like something she'd already done once that day.

Otskai nudged her mare forward to the front of the line beside Beaver Tail as Shoshone lodges appeared ahead of them. Maybe this second village would be the place they'd find her cousin.

Two men stepped from the camp, one with two braids hanging down his back, a few white hairs showing even from this distance. The other was younger, but her focus honed on the one who'd caught her attention first.

From this distance, she couldn't see whether he carried a burn mark on his face, but the feathers hanging from one of the braids were striped, like those of the hawk. Surely there were many braves who wore their hair that way, with those black-and-white striped feathers. But Twin Elk had worn that same striped quill all the time.

She kept her voice low so only Beaver Tail could hear. "I think I know the one, the older."

The men stood a few strides out from the camp, waiting for

them to approach. They surely saw the women in their group and knew this wasn't a war party.

More people appeared among the lodges, and Otskai strained to find her cousin's familiar form. Watkeuse was taller than she was, with broad shoulders and a strong bearing, features that always made Otskai feel even younger than the three years that separated them. Regardless of the age difference, with all of the brothers in their lodge, they'd connected as fast friends.

Had Watkeuse also found a place here? If she'd stayed with these people almost three years, she must have.

A husband. Surely she had one by now. That possibility had seemed distant enough to push aside before.

But now, faced with a camp full of lodges and a host of braves standing among them, along with women and children who'd come out to gawk at the newcomers, it seemed impossible Watkeuse hadn't found a man among so many. She couldn't stay as a guest of the chief's wife forever. She would need a husband to provide her a lodge of her own.

As they rode closer, the man with the hawk feathers became clear, his features more familiar with every step, the red marring the right side of his face now evident. "The older is Twin Elk, one of those Watkeuse left with."

Beaver Tail gave a slight nod but kept his focus forward in the way braves usually did. She turned her gaze to Twin Elk to see if he recognized her.

Beaver Tail reined in a half-dozen strides from Twin Elk and the younger man. Twin Elk's eyes shifted from Beaver and her, then back to Beaver. He'd probably already looked over the rest of the group. When his eyes flicked to her once more, certainty pressed inside her. He must have recognized her.

Beaver Tail greeted the man in the Shoshone tongue. Was there any language this man didn't know? His words weren't fluid but certainly understandable. Better than she could have managed.

After Twin Elk returned the greeting, Beaver began his inquiry. "We are looking for a woman from the Nimiipuu camp across the mountains. Her name is Watkeuse, and her cousin wishes to visit with her." Beaver Tail nodded to Otskai, and Twin Elk glanced at her again before returning to the Blackfoot brave.

Beaver Tail was wise in calling this only a visit. If Watkeuse had married into this tribe, they wouldn't willingly turn her over. And Twin Elk might remember Otskai as her cousin.

Twin Elk's brows lowered in thought. But it was the man beside him who drew Otskai's notice.

At Watkeuse's name, he'd stiffened. It was the only movement he made, but something about it snagged her focus. She tried to read his expression, but his face had become a mask.

Before, he'd seemed simply a companion as Twin Elk came to greet them and learn their purpose in coming. But now his manner made him seem like a guard. Maybe not so much to keep them out as to protect something inside. Watkeuse, most likely.

Had her cousin married this man? She ran her gaze over him once more, trying to see him as Watkeuse would. In their younger days, they'd giggled about a few of the young men around the village. But as they came of age, Watkeuse had begun to scorn the braves they grew up with.

Of course, her father hadn't contracted her to marry as he had done with Otskai. Maybe deep inside, he'd known Watkeuse would refuse.

This fellow wasn't like the young braves Watkeuse had shared an interest in early on. They'd been sure of themselves, cocky. In truth, their confidence had probably drawn her cousin more than anything else.

But as her own assurance had grown, she hadn't seemed to need the attentions of men any longer.

What was it about this fellow that had drawn Watkeuse's notice? He didn't seem especially sure of himself, certainly not cocky.

Twin Elk motioned them forward, turning toward the camp. The murmur of his voice sounded as he spoke to the younger man, but Otskai couldn't make out the words. The fellow strode into the camp to one of the lodges on the second row from the edge. Otskai nudged her mare forward as Beaver Tail did the same, but she kept her gaze on the tipi the man had ducked inside.

When they reached the row of outer lodges, they dismounted. Adam and Joel stepped to Caleb's side to help him climb down from his mare. Otskai was usually the one to hover near in case an extra set of hands was helpful as he found his balance with his walking sticks, but Joel took her place this time. A good thing, since River Boy sprinted toward her the moment Elan set him on the ground.

Otskai sent another glance toward the lodge the brave had disappeared inside, then turned her focus to her son. She took a firm grip on his hand. "Stay with me."

Just as she looked toward the dwelling once more, the door flap lifted and the brave stepped out again. Another figure came behind him, and Otskai's heart lifted at the familiar outline.

Watkeuse paused in front of the lodge and stared their direction. The moment she recognized Otskai, her entire bearing changed.

She didn't walk forward, she ran. The brave who'd gone to get her stepped out of her way, as did every other person and dog in front of her. So much joy lit her cousin's face, it spread warmth through Otskai's soul.

She started forward, then dropped her son's hand as her

cousin flung strong arms around her and squeezed tight, spinning them a half turn in the process.

"Otskai. My sister." Watkeuse's laughing words expressed the same fervent energy she'd always used to embrace life. Whether joy or anger or heartache, she flung herself into the feeling with every part of her.

Otskai clung as tight as her cousin did, giving herself for just a moment to the sweet feeling and scent and memory of her cousin, her dearest friend. The one person she'd confided in when the days grew hardest after her parents died and again in the season leading up to her marriage to Motsqueh.

Then, with her usual decisive manner, Watkeuse pulled away, keeping one hand on Otskai's arm as she leaned forward to see the lad hiding partway behind her. "Who is this big boy?" Watkeuse bent low and smiled. "I'm your aunt, and I've been waiting a long time to finally meet you."

Otskai took her son's arm and pulled him forward. "This is your aunt Watkeuse." Her cousin had always called them sisters, probably because they'd both needed that tighter connection. Watkeuse had struggled under the oppression of her chieftain father and four older brothers, and Otskai had had no one left, save the extended family who took her into their lodge.

Watkeuse doted on the boy until she gained a grin from him. Then she rose with a satisfied smile and scanned the group standing a few steps behind Otskai. "You all must stay with me. I have plenty of room. It might be tight with so many, but we'll be merry."

She turned and spoke to the group of Shoshone who had gathered behind her. Several half-grown boys trotted forward to take their horses.

Soon, they had gathered around the outside cook fire in front of Watkeuse's lodge. The brave who'd gone to retrieve her was among those nearby, along with chief Twin Elk and his wife. The woman's long braids contained more gray hairs than when they'd come to the Nimiipuu village, but she still possessed the same outgoing, almost-pushy manner. Where Watkeuse was simply exuberant and confident in her actions, this woman was brash.

Watkeuse hadn't introduced the brave yet, hadn't made introductions to anyone. The man certainly watched her, but Otskai couldn't read his expression. Fondness yes, even a little—jealousy maybe? Now that the two could be seen in the same glance, she could imagine them paired together, even though he didn't fit Watkeuse's taste from her younger days.

But...they didn't quite seem a pair. Watkeuse didn't look at him with any sign of possession or affection. But then, Otskai couldn't imagine that expression on her cousin's face. Watkeuse was too much of a free spirit to be pressed into the mold of diligent squaw.

Watkeuse finally made introductions, announcing the man as White Owl but still didn't speak of his relation to her. Maybe that lack meant there truly was nothing between them. Had she secured a lodge and lived as a single woman among these people for almost three years?

It didn't seem likely, but if anyone could manage the feat, Watkeuse could.

Otskai sat with River Boy in her lap and her cousin at her side. Her son's eyes had begun to droop, probably the only reason he sat without squirming for so long.

As the men spoke of the weather and the mountain crossing, Watkeuse turned to her and kept her voice low. "How are my parents? And the boys? Has Isekiukse's wife given him little ones yet? I'm sure they finally had the marriage ceremony for Ziekse and his intended." Watkeuse rattled off a few more questions about her family before giving Otskai a chance to respond.

She gave only the answers to Watkeuse's questions, not the reason they'd come to this village. That would be better saved for a time when the two of them were truly alone. She would only have one good chance to convince her cousin, and she'd best plan the setting well.

After Watkeuse seemed satisfied with Otskai's remarks, she sent a meaningful glance around the group. "And what are you doing with these? Has Motsqueh finally given you a season to yourself? Or did you sneak away while he was gone on the hunt?"

A pain pressed in Otskai's chest. Her cousin didn't know. She worked to school her emotions. "He has been gone more than two years. A Crow arrow pierced his chest." She laid her hand over her heart, the place where the lifeblood had seeped from her husband. She'd not been there to see it, but her uncle had told her all.

Watkeuse sobered, her eyes darkening with pain. "I'm sorry, my sister." The words were barely a murmur, but their feeling soothed a balm over Otskai's heart.

For long moments, silence settled between them. The men still talked, but they spoke both Shoshone and sign, which made it easy for Otskai to push their voices away. She could speak the language but had to think through each word.

Watkeuse's gaze settled on River Boy, who'd rested his cheek on Otskai's chest, his eyes closed and breathing even. He could surely hear the beat of her heart, just as he had in her womb. His sweet face sent a warmth to wrap around her, and love rose within her so strong, it nearly pressed her breath away.

"He is beautiful." Watkeuse's voice was soft, and the truth of her words sank deep within Otskai. "Did his father meet him?"

Otskai shook her head, keeping her focus on her son as the sting of tears rushed in. She loved her freedom, but it wasn't worth the death of a man. Motsqueh should have been able to meet his son. The boy should have known his father.

But she had to press that line of thought away before it took over. She could change nothing now.

After a moment, Watkeuse lifted her gaze back to Otskai. "You did not say why you travel with these."

How could she answer without raising her cousin's suspicion? "They were coming across the mountains and invited me along. I wanted to see you." Nothing in those words lied, but they formed a false picture.

The laughter of small voices sounded from behind them, then a girl cried "Mama," in the Shoshone tongue. Watkeuse turned at the young voice as though she recognized it.

Otskai followed her gaze to a girl of maybe five or six winters. The child had been running toward them, a younger boy and girl trailing behind her. When the first girl's gaze took in their group, she dropped to a walk.

Watkeuse held out a hand for the child to approach.

A tumble of thoughts spun in Otskai's mind. Surely the girl hadn't been calling Watkeuse her mother. Maybe she'd been looking for her parent and was coming to see if Watkeuse knew where that woman was. There was no way her cousin could have given birth to a babe who'd grown to this age. Even if she'd been with child when she left, not quite three years had passed.

The girl neared, and Watkeuse took her hand, drawing her down to her knees between them. With a sweet smile, Watkeuse turned to Otskai and spoke in Nimiiputimpt. "I'd like you to meet Pop-pank. My daughter. "

CHAPTER 20

Caleb studied Otskai as she spoke with her cousin. When Watkeuse drew the young girl into their group and spoke again to Otskai, the draining of color in her features was almost as bad as when they'd faced the rushing river.

Something wasn't right here. Otskai had said nothing about Watkeuse being with child, and if he had his timing right, there was no way she could've given birth to this one anyway.

As the two women talked more, Otskai regained some of her color and spoke to the girl. He wasn't close enough to understand, even if he knew the Shoshone language. It seemed like that was another tongue he would need to learn. But first Nimiiputimpt and the language of signs that all the tribes spoke. One more undertaking he'd need the Lord's help to accomplish.

But even as Otskai continued visiting with the woman and girl, her features held a tightness that hadn't been there before. This girl would be a complication.

How was Watkeuse connected with her? The child must belong to one of the families here. Had the woman and girl simply grown close? He still hadn't worked out whether Watkeuse was married to the brave who kept watching her.

Sometimes he thought that likely, but he'd not seen a particular affection for him in Watkeuse's manner.

Caleb flicked a glance toward the man again. As before, the brave was watching Watkeuse, and the look in his eyes...

Recognition slipped through Caleb. He knew that look, the longing in the man's gaze. Unrequited love.

That feeling had grown a little more in his own chest as each day passed on this journey. The kiss he and Otskai had shared four days ago had shifted the sensation. His love wasn't quite as unrequited anymore. Otskai had planted a hope that maybe she felt the same.

Although what she would do about it, he wasn't sure yet. They'd not had any time alone since then. And he couldn't quite put a finger on whether she was forcing the separation or it was happenstance.

At least around this cooking fire, he knew what was happening. This man wanted to be with Watkeuse, but she didn't return his affections. *I feel your pain, fella.*

Whether the man deserved her or not was yet to be determined, but at least Watkeuse didn't seem to have the connection of a man keeping her in this place.

He sent another glance at Otskai. She was smiling as she said something to her cousin. But when her gaze dipped to the girl, he couldn't miss the worry in her eyes, even across the campfire.

The knot in his belly pulled tighter. *Work all things together for good, Lord.* They'd found Watkeuse, but he had a feeling they'd not fought the toughest battle yet.

"You must tell me all about the white man."

Heat flew up Otskai's neck, but she tried to hide her reaction to her cousin's words. She knew exactly which white man Watkeuse spoke of, but she couldn't help goading a little.

"Which *soyapo* do you mean?" She kept her voice innocent as they strolled in the early morning mist. Elan had taken River Boy and Pop-pank for a walk so Otskai and Watkeuse could have a few moments alone.

One corner of Watkeuse's mouth tipped up as her eyes sparkled. "The one your son already loves as his father. The one who looks at you as though he would scrape the thorns from the huckleberry vines just so they won't poke you."

The words lit inside Otskai like a flame to dry tinder. She shouldn't have pressed her cousin if she didn't want the truth. Still, the flame was searing her cheeks and ears.

She kept her focus forward. "You probably mean Caleb. He's been so much help with River Boy."

"Tell me of him. Where did he come from? How long have you known him?"

These questions she could answer without turning red. "He came with the other white men and the Blackfoot to our village at the beginning of winter. They left for a few moons, then returned. It was then they asked me to travel with them." She had to find a way to tell Watkeuse of the mission her father had sent them on. This walk was her chance to make the request. But maybe there was a better way to approach the topic.

Watkeuse had been watching her as silence settled between them, but now she turned her focus forward. Hopefully her thoughts wouldn't make her imagine more existed between Otskai and Caleb than really did. Maybe Otskai should simply tell her how she felt about Caleb.

Yet she didn't know herself. Caleb was a good man. A man she could trust, she was almost certain of that. A man she could love, if she let herself. But marriage was simply a form of bondage, and she couldn't reconcile herself to becoming another man's servant.

Did that mean she had to put distance between her and Caleb? Send him away as soon as they returned to her village? The thought pressed so hard in her chest she could barely breathe. Yet there was nothing else to do. If he chose to stay near, she would be even more miserable, having him so close yet forcing distance between them.

"I think it can be good. Sometimes." Watkeuse's voice came softly.

Otskai sorted through what her cousin might be speaking of. Did she mean the affections of a man? Affection could be good. Probably. But affection was not marriage. Belonging to a man was a very different thing.

Watkeuse turned to her, a question in her gaze.

Otskai scrambled for a response. "What can?"

Her cousin's face softened. "Marriage to a worthy man. When his heart is good and there is love, when you choose to hold onto that love, no matter what comes."

Questions slipped through Otskai, but she couldn't grasp them enough to speak. The image Watkeuse's words painted sounded wonderful, but not real.

"I have seen it," Watkeuse said. "I have seen two people who married because they chose to. They committed to keep the affection and to put the other first. Life is not always pleasant, but the hard times made their love stronger. It was beautiful to watch." A glimmer of emotion filled Watkeuse's gaze with those last words.

Maybe thoughts of those friends brought that look. Or maybe the desire to have what Watkeuse spoke of for herself.

A yearning pressed hard in Otskai. She could imagine a life like that with Caleb. He made her better. Each challenge they'd gone through made her want to turn to him in the trial. And he was always there. His solid presence, the strength of his sureness. Her rock when everything else was being washed away.

Heat stung her eyes. If she let herself think of him, she would not be able to stay strong for the conversation ahead.

Better to turn the questions to Watkeuse. "Who were these people?"

A sadness filtered over her cousin's expression. "Pop-pank's parents. Her mother became my good friend here." Her mouth curved in a small smile. "My Otskai." Then she pressed a hand to her chest. "Their love was beautiful and showed me what I had always wanted."

Watkeuse faced forward again, and her brow furrowed. "There was always something missing with the men my father wanted me to marry. When I saw my friend here with her husband, I realized what I wanted. What I wouldn't settle for lacking. He adored her, and when she was apart from him, as we picked berries or dug for camas roots, I would see her smiling, smile that brightened everything around her, just because she was thinking of him."

She halted and spun to face Otskai. "I want that. I want to love a man that way. But I will not settle for someone who doesn't feel every bit the same."

The fierceness on her cousin's face almost made Otskai smile. Maybe this was her chance to find the answer to another question. "White Owl? You don't feel that way about him?"

Watkeuse's expression shifted again, but it was such a mixture of emotion, Otskai couldn't decipher it. "I... No. I don't." But an unspoken...*think so* hovered in the air. Maybe it wasn't the passion Watkeuse sought, but there was emotion there.

Otskai kept her voice gentle. "I think he feels that way about you. At least, he admires you a great deal."

She lifted a single shoulder as her gaze roamed the fresh growth along the path. "He is Pop-pank's uncle. Her father's brother."

That was an opening she shouldn't pass by. "Will we meet

Pop-pank's parents soon?" They hadn't been there the day before. The girl had slept in Watkeuse's lodge, on her own little pallet beside Watkeuse's.

Lines feathered the edges of Watkeuse's eyes as she lifted her gaze to the distant mountains. "Her parents died. Killed by the sickness brought by the French trappers. She is mine now. My daughter."

Watkeuse tipped her gaze to Otskai, showing the red rimming her eyes. "I promised her mother I would raise her with the same love she was surrounded with before. The same happiness." Her voice cracked on the last word, and she pressed her mouth shut as she faced forward again.

For long moments, they strolled in quiet. This was not a turn Otskai had expected, though she should have known there was more between her cousin and the child from the affection between them.

What now? How did this girl affect the possibility of Watkeuse returning with them? Maybe it didn't have to. Pop-pank could simply travel along.

As though she'd been following Otskai's thoughts, Watkeuse stopped and turned to face her. "Tell me now, sister. Why is it you've come? The truth."

This was the moment. The time to share all, but she had to be careful. She met her cousin's gaze. "Your father longs for you. Both your parents. But your father has mourned you ever since you left."

Watkeuse raised one brow higher than the other. "I am dead to him then?"

Otskai had to hold in a snort. Of course her cousin would take her words further than she meant. "I can promise you are very much alive in his mind. He sent us to find you. To learn how you are and to bring you back so he can see for himself." She softened her tone and added a bit of pleading. "He loves you, sister. More than you might imagine. He worries."

Lines fanned across Watkeuse's brow, and she shifted her focus to the distance, somewhere over Otskai's shoulder.

There was a time Otskai would have known what she was thinking. Would have been able to follow the line of her ponderings. But she didn't know enough about her cousin's life now. She could only answer to what little she did. "Pop-pank should come too, of course. Your parents will love to meet her."

Silence settled again and tightened with each heartbeat. Something else was warring within her cousin. Was it the brave? Pop-pank's uncle?

At last, Watkeuse refocused on her. "What else? There's something more that brought you to me. Are my parents ill? My brothers? Why have you come now, when your son is still young and the journey hard?" Then her expression softened. "I'm glad you've come. But I need to know everything."

Otskai released a long breath. She may as well tell it all. There was no reason to hold back about the tomahawk her uncle had promised to return in exchange for bringing Watkeuse home. She just had to make sure Watkeuse saw the love behind the mission, not just the strategy.

"My uncle has longed for your return from the day you left. He only let you go because you begged it of him. But it didn't stop his worry or the loss both your parents felt when you left. He knew you wouldn't come home merely because he asked." She gave Watkeuse a sad smile. "You may think he doesn't understand you, but he knew this. You needed your freedom. You would demand it."

Watkeuse nodded, but her mouth formed a slim line as she waited for more.

"Meksem, the Nimiipuu warrior from the Pikunin camp north of ours had traded her prize tomahawk to my uncle in exchange for one of his best horses. The white man she's to marry learned of the trade and wishes to return it to her. He asked my uncle what he could do to win back the tomahawk. I think my uncle suspected sending me with these white men might be the only way you would be willing to come home.

"So he asked Adam to find you. To bring you home, if you would come. I agreed to accompany them to make introductions. And because I wanted to see you myself, and I wanted you to meet my son." All true, although not the entire truth. That last part at least.

A sigh leaked from her cousin that might have contained all the frustration that had built toward her parents through her eight and twenty winters. "Of course my father would hold these two strangers' happiness over me to make me come back."

Tension twisted tighter in Otskai's chest. "He's desperate to see you again, Watkeuse. It was an act of love. I never realized the depth of his heart for you until I saw him grieve your absence."

Her cousin's mouth returned to that thin line, but her eyes were shuttered in thought.

Otskai held her tongue, forcing herself to wait. Watkeuse needed time to process everything.

At last, her cousin threw up a hand. "I will go to him. Poppank and I both. They should know her, you're right." Then her eyes narrowed on Otskai. "But I will not stay. I will tell him to give this man the tomahawk, and I will see my brothers and their families. Then I will return to my home here."

Otskai held in a laugh, but a bit of the sound slipped out, half strangled. Hopefully, this would fulfill Adam's mission. Watkeuse probably could get her father to give back the tomahawk, but that wouldn't lay to rest the troubled feelings in their family.

Once Maksem had her tomahawk back, the band of friends would be on their way.

Caleb along with them.

A weight pressed so hard on her chest, she couldn't draw breath. Her lungs ached. No, that was her heart. How would she ever watch him go? And River Boy. How could she let his sweet little heart be broken that way?

Watkeuse's gaze turned shrewd. "Unless you don't want me to. You want me to be stubborn so your white man has longer to make up his mind about you?" Her mouth tipped up at the corners in true Watkeuse fashion.

Otskai forced in a tiny bit of air and shook her head. "Get Adam back the tomahawk. It's not fair when it means so much to Meksem."

Otskai would have to manage the pain of Caleb's leaving herself. She'd always known getting too close to others brought pain. Only in this case, it was the leaving that would hurt most, not the staying.

CHAPTER 21

"Why are you ignoring him?"

Otskai squeezed her eyes shut against her cousin's nagging question. Three days they'd stayed in this Shoshone town as Watkeuse prepared for the journey and Caleb rested his injured leg.

Three days that had given Otskai ample time to remember how much of a bossy, overbearing elder sister her cousin could be. Like a beaver gnawing at a log, she nipped and bit and scraped until sometimes Otskai wanted to swing around and backhand her.

Instead, she let out a breath and reached for the patient tone. "I'm not ignoring him. I'm simply going about my day. There's nothing between us, Watkeuse." Not much anyway. If she stayed away from Caleb long enough, maybe what there had been would have fizzled out by the time they reached home.

"That's not what he said."

Otskai spun away from the bowl she was washing and stared at her cousin. "You didn't ask him." Surely not even Watkeuse was bold enough to meddle so.

Her cousin raised her brows, her expression making it

impossible to tell whether she'd done the heinous act or was simply goading a response from Otskai.

"Watkeuse." The word came out more like a growl than Otskai had meant.

But her cousin only chuckled and waved the warning aside. "I came to tell you I'm ready to leave when the rest of you are. You, uh..." She threw a glance back to camp where Caleb and the other men were speaking with a few of the village elders. "You might want to check with your brave before we choose when to set out though. I haven't seen his leg today, but it didn't look so well yesterday."

Otskai followed the look toward the lodges as her belly cramped tighter. They'd stayed in the Shoshone village to give Caleb the rest he needed. His leg had to be much better before they started back. The journey would provide more than enough challenge for his fragile limb.

"Why don't you go check on him now? I'll finish here and watch the little ones." Watkeuse motioned toward where Poppank and River Boy poured cups and bowls of water from one container to the next. The girl possessed a vivid imagination and kept up a steady chatter that seemed to mesmerize her son. He didn't know the Shoshone tongue, but the language of the innocent didn't seem to need the spoken word.

Still...though the two sat away from the river's edge, she couldn't leave her son so close to the water. This little pool where she was doing the washing seemed serene. But outside this calm space, the river rushed in a vicious flow.

She laid the clean bowl in the stack with the others, then pushed to her feet. "I'll take River Boy with me."

"Leave him." Watkeuse's tone was more command than suggestion. She propped a hand on her hip and gave Otskai her big sister look. "I won't take my eyes off him. And Pop-pank is a little afraid of the water. She won't let him near it."

Otskai swallowed down the fear that tried to rise up her

throat in a hard knot. She'd told her cousin of her son's penchant for water. And of the times she'd nearly lost him. Watkeuse might be stubborn, but that determination had always made her watchful.

Maybe Otskai could leave River Boy in her care for just a few minutes while she went to speak with Caleb. If he was still with the other men, her son's energy would not be a welcome interruption. For that matter, perhaps she, too, should wait until he wasn't busy.

"Go. He'll be glad to see you, and we need to make a decision about when to leave." Again, Watkeuse had listened in on her thoughts.

With a nod, she started toward the village. "I won't be long."

When she rounded one of the outer lodges to see the front of Watkeuse's home, the men were no longer gathered around the outside fire.

Only one man remained there. His long body lay stretched out on the grass, probably enjoying the faint warmth of the early spring sun.

Caleb's eyes were closed, but when she took a step nearer, they opened, and he turned his head her way. The smile curving his mouth as his gaze locked on her made her entire body spring to life.

He worked himself upright, the hesitation in his movement proof that the claw marks still pained him, at least some. He patted the ground beside him and spoke in the Nimiippu language, as he often did. "Want to sit?" His cadence was getting better.

She sank down on the grass at his side, her gaze wandering to his injured foot. She switched to English to make the conversation easier for him. "How are you mending?"

He reached down and brushed some grass off his knee, drawing her focus up his arm and to his face. The handsome face that even now made her heart race.

With a scrunch of his nose, he tipped his head. "Better."

She forced her focus back down to the ankle. He'd wrapped it to a stick again, but this one looked a bit smoother, probably more comfortable than the rough pole they'd used on the trail.

With the binding, she couldn't tell exactly how swollen the joint was. It didn't look to be a normal size though.

"Maybe you should spend more time soaking it in the river. The cold water seems to help, no?"

Again the wrinkle of his nose. "I should, I suppose. It's just lonely down there when everyone else is here."

She tried to fight a guilty blush from rising. She should have invited him when she took the dishes for washing. If she hadn't been working so hard to avoid him, she would have thought of that.

"Come to the river now. My cousin is working there, and the little ones are playing." She started to rise, but he laid a hand on her arm, stilling her.

She forced her gaze to his face. He wore that smile that must have gotten him out of every scrape when he was a boy. Even now, it softened her to jelly. "Sit with me a few minutes longer. Can you? Then I'll go down to the river."

When he looked at her that way, his warm eyes dancing, her head nodded before she even gave it permission.

She settled in beside him again, and his hand lingered on her arm for another heartbeat. He looked as though he might plan to keep it there, or run his fingers down to entwine with hers. Her heart pulsed harder at the thought, at the longing that swept through her.

But he pulled away.

The loss made it hard to keep her composure. They'd not spoken of the kiss. Not really spoken of anything between them.

And she wanted desperately to keep the silence. She wanted it almost as much as she wanted him to pull her close right there and press his mouth to hers with the strength that ignited fire inside her.

But that couldn't happen. In her mind, she pulled away from him. Maybe her body did the same too, for he swung his gaze up to hers, a question in his eyes. Perhaps even a bit of hurt.

This wasn't fair to him. After the way she'd responded to his kiss, she had to tell him why nothing could come of it.

But he spoke before she could come to terms with that thought. "Has your cousin said when she'll be ready to leave?"

Otskai let out a breath and dipped her chin. "She's prepared to go when we're ready. It's up to us to plan the day."

He nodded. "I'll speak with Beaver and the others. I suspect we could head out as early as tomorrow."

Her gaze jerked to his face. "But your leg... You need more time."

His jaw locked, and something flared in his gaze. It wasn't anger. Maybe frustration. She'd seen that hint of bullheaded stubbornness before too. Mostly from her cousin.

"I'm fine. I can leave tomorrow morning. The leg doesn't hurt."

If Motsqueh had been the one saying those words, she would've bit her tongue and complied with his wishes. Or rather his demands, for there was never a doubt he expected his commands to be obeyed.

But this wasn't Motsqueh. She'd not subjected herself to Caleb's rule. And leaving so soon would make his journey so much harder, maybe even stop the ankle from healing the way it should.

He could be stubborn if he wanted to, but so could she.

Raising her chin, she met his gaze. "If you think you're ready to leave, unwrap your ankle and show it to me. Let me see that the break is healed and its size matches the other. I won't let you be foolish. I won't let your stubborn pride hurt you even more."

Caleb's eyes grew a tiny bit wider, yet no anger darkened his features. In fact, his gaze seemed to brighten. Maybe even…twinkle.

The corners of his mouth crept up, and when he spoke, his voice had softened. "I like it when you speak your mind. I like knowing what you really think." His tone eased over her like a gentle touch.

As much as she tried to hold her ire, she couldn't help sinking into the pleasure of him.

As the connection between them held, he looked as if he might lean forward and kiss her again.

Her stomach fluttered at the thought even as her chest tightened. She would let him. But she couldn't. Yet every part of her wanted to.

But she couldn't.

Maybe he read the resolution on her face, for he didn't kiss her.

Instead, his gaze slipped down to his injured leg. "Maybe one more day. I really am a lot better. The swelling is mostly gone. One more day to let it settle completely, and I'll be ready."

She followed his focus to the limb, though she could see nothing with the bandage. She'd have to look for herself when he soaked it.

But for now, she nodded and started to rise. "Come to the river now."

"Otskai." Something in Caleb's tone gave her pause, and she again turned back to him.

His gaze was so gentle, yet…uncertain. Not something she was accustomed to seeing in his eyes. Her belly formed a knot as she waited for what he would say next.

"We've not spoken of…" His throat worked as he seemed to be struggling for the right words, even though he spoke English.

Her own insides jumbled tighter as his topic came clear. Did they have to speak of the kiss? She needed to tell him that nothing could come between them. But not now. She wasn't ready for the connection between them to end.

"I need you to know how important you've become to me. You and River Boy both."

The earnestness in his gaze only intensified her panic, like his words gripped her around the throat and squeezed. She wasn't ready for this conversation. Speaking of this thing between them meant she would have to tell him nothing could come of it.

And that would stop everything. Stop his gentle touch, the tender look when his eyes met hers and even when he looked at her son.

She started to shake her head.

But his hand on her arm gave a gentle squeeze. "Wait. Please. I just want to say you don't have to be in a hurry to decide whether you feel anything for me. I'll wait. Take as long as you need to. I'm not going anywhere."

His words jumbled in her mind like a wind swirled them, and she wasn't even sure she understood him clearly. Panic welled higher in her throat. She simply had to get away.

So she stood, pulling her arm from his, then turned and nearly sprinted toward the river. Never before had she run to water for safety. But this time, she would rather face the foaming tempest of surging waves than the hurt she'd just caused in the eyes of this man she cared for more than she was willing to face.

CALEB WANTED TO KICK SOMETHING. Hard. With his broken leg.

But he settled for pounding a fist on the ground. Why had he pushed her? He'd known from the moment he first asked Otskai to sit beside him that she wasn't ready to talk about the kiss. But he'd persisted. Not until he started to bring it up did he finally allow himself to see the panic in her eyes.

He'd been a blind fool for thinking that telling her of his feelings would ease her concerns about the kiss. He was surely the dumbest lovesick sot who ever lived.

His gaze rose to the place where she'd disappeared around the corner of the lodge at the outer edge of camp. Maybe she'd gone back to the river to help with the work there. Or maybe even to retrieve her son. He was surprised she'd left the boy in someone else's care so close to the water.

She must trust her cousin a great deal.

Would it make things worse for her if he hobbled to that place to soak his leg? He'd promised he would as soon as they finished talking, but he had a feeling his presence wouldn't be welcome right now.

But then, the river ran a long distance. He could find a spot upstream from Otskai, out of her way. Maybe near the waterfall. The rushing flow would be a nice sound to fall asleep to. His body seemed to need more and more rest these days. He'd been about to doze off when Otskai had approached a few minutes ago, and part of him longed to return to that sleepy haze.

Reaching for the walking sticks, he struggled up to his knees, then to standing. His breaths came harder by the time he stood upright, and his ankle had resumed the thudding ache he'd finally managed to get rid of.

He started forward, nodding to an older woman who sat outside a nearby lodge, scraping a small animal hide.

Her grin revealed uneven teeth, but beautiful eyes were wreathed with deep smile lines. The joy reflected on her face must bring a smile to God every time.

Hobbling on, he left the camp behind and set out across the

longer field to the falls. A footpath had been worn that direction.

He sent a glance toward the quiet pool where Otskai was probably working. Several figures were there, but with the trees and brush around them, he couldn't make out enough to recognize people.

Even with the fur padding he'd wrapped around the top ends of the walking sticks, they dug in under his arms. But he kept moving.

Spray rose up from the waterfall, casting dampness into the air around the place. The sun was behind him now, and when sunlight was positioned behind the spray, it probably made all sorts of beautiful rainbows.

When he reached the pool at the base of the falls, he had to drop to his haunches and slide down the embankment to get close enough to the water. Once settled at the river's edge, he unwrapped the bandage that bound his ankle to the two braces French had fastened.

With the injury bared, he pulled up both trouser legs to study the ankles side-by-side. The broken one was still a little bigger, but nothing compared to how it had swollen on the trail. If he spent a while today soaking it in this water, then several more times tomorrow, he should be ready to ride again by the following morning.

He eased his injured foot into the water, sucking in a breath at the first frigid touch. Within a minute or two, the limb would be numb. But until then, he had to force in steady breaths as he situated the ankle under the surface.

At last, his foot adjusted to the icy water enough that he could relax. Lying back on the ground, he pushed out a long breath, consciously relaxing each part of his body as he took in another lungful of cool air. He let his eyes drift shut.

Otskai's face filled his mind, her beautiful eyes wide as they'd been when she pulled away from him minutes before.

She's out of my control, Lord. You'll have to work on her. Draw her to You. Soften her heart to me. Help me be what You need me to be until then. Give me patience, Lord.

And strength for whatever lies ahead.

CHAPTER 22

Otskai dropped to her knees beside her cousin at the river's edge. Watkeuse had finished the dishes and begun washing the stack of clothing she'd brought down earlier.

A glance behind her showed Pop-pank and River Boy crawling through the grass. The two seemed to be pretending to sneak up on something. Pop-pank was motioning for River Boy to duck lower and crawl on his elbows, but her son shuffled on hands and feet like a baby bear, his little bottom rising high.

Even with all the turmoil in her heart, she couldn't help a smile at the sight. If she could protect his innocence forever, keep him just the way he was now, she would.

At least…she would consider it. His constant activity still exhausted her, but thankfully, he had someone to play with here. Pop-pank seemed to enjoy mothering him, maybe a bit like Watkeuse had been with Otskai when they were little.

She brought her focus back to their work in time to see Watkeuse watching her. "They play well together, eh?"

Otskai nodded and worked for a normal smile. "A little like we use to."

Watkeuse must have picked up on something not right in her tone or her expression, for she studied her.

Otskai reached for a buckskin tunic, one that must be Poppank's, if the size and multitude of decorations were any sign.

"What did he say to you?" Watkeuse's tone nosed in just like a bossy elder sister.

Otskai forced her face not to reveal her frustration as she scrubbed at a dark spot in the leather. "He said he should be ready to go after two sleeps. He will come down to the river soon to soak his leg in the cold water."

Her cousin's gaze pressed into her, but Otskai didn't reward her nosiness by revealing that anything bothered her. At least she tried not to.

"And that is why you're tensed like a rabbit ready to jump away?"

Gripping the buckskin tighter, she rubbed two sections harder. With her hands underwater, her cousin wouldn't see the whiteness of her grip. "I'm not running away."

But she had. She'd fled from Caleb faster than that frightened rabbit. Why hadn't she simply looked him in the eye and told him her decision?

He wasn't cruel. She'd never seen him lose his temper. He might rile on occasion, as anyone did. But he never let his anger run free. Not once had he pointed out one of her faults. He'd encouraged and waited with an amount of patience she wouldn't have managed. Even in the midst of his pain, he still thought of others.

But that was the problem. All those qualities that had stolen her heart and won her over so completely would be there still when she told him what she knew he didn't want to hear.

Being a man, he probably wouldn't show any pain her words caused. He would be kind. Maybe he'd tell her not to worry about him. He might walk away as she asked, simply because that was best for her and River Boy, even if he didn't want to. Caleb was simply that good.

And she didn't want him to walk away.

She pulled the tunic from the water and squeezed the liquid from it while she admitted the truth to herself. She wanted to cling to every scrap of his attention she could garner.

As *selfless* as he was, she was even more *selfish*. The only thing that demanded she pushed him away was her craving for independence. Was that need so much more important than the happiness Watkeuse had spoken of the other day? Could she really find that joy with Caleb?

That old oppressive weight settled around her. Her eyes began to twitch as the memory of Motsqueh sank over her. He'd never hit her, only smothered her under the weight of his expectations. Of his demands. She couldn't go back to that. Every part of her wanted to spring away like a rabbit fleeing the predator. Maybe a life with Caleb wouldn't be so difficult, but fear rose up strong within her. She couldn't risk it.

"Otskai?"

Something in her cousin's tone made Otskai look up. But Watkeuse wasn't looking at her, she was scanning around them. Then behind.

"Pop-pank?" Watkeuse straightened as she peered in the bushes behind them.

Otskai lurched to her feet, her mind catching up with a rush of fear. "River Boy?" She spun to search the area around them, straining for some sign of motion. "Come to me, son. Where are you?"

Nothing. Not even the flick of a leaf or the sway of grass. The rushing of the river was so loud, the sound overpowered any noise the children might be making.

She started toward the last spot she'd seen them, where they'd been crawling in the grass. Maybe they were hiding.

But no.

Every time her son went missing, she almost always found him going toward the river. She spun back to the water. Why had she taken her eyes off him so close to this deadly expanse?

Her heart roared through her chest, pounding in her ears as she studied the river. So many rocks, and each one made her chest lurch as her mind saw River Boy in its shape. One, the dark stringy locks of his water-soaked head. Another, the hump of his back as he floated lifelessly away.

But none were her son, only rocks solid enough to knock him senseless if the powerful current slammed him against them.

"River Boy!" She screamed his name, her heart rending with fear as she struggled to breathe. Struggled to think.

Which way would he have gone? Maybe her cousin would know, but Watkeuse had started back toward the camp. Probably looking for them there.

But Otskai couldn't leave the river without searching. She focused upstream first, her eyes moving over every rock, every change in the water's coloring. Her feet followed the path, leaping through the grass as she strained to see anything that might be a person. A little boy.

Her son.

Caleb's God, if you're there, protect him. Not for me but for Caleb. For my innocent son. Don't let him die in this river.

Panic churned in her throat, cutting off her breath. But she kept her gaze honed on the river as she ran.

There was nothing. No sign of her son. But the roaring had grown louder and louder, blocking out every other sound. The water churned with even more violence than before, rushing in frothy waves.

She glanced farther upriver, just in case she might catch sight of a young boy flailing. Could he have come this far?

The sight there speared through her like a tomahawk slicing from her throat to her chest.

A waterfall.

Her feet wouldn't move, but her hungry gaze clambered up the curtain of water. The height of the falls rose taller than she was. High enough that a boy dropping from that level would be smashed if he landed on a rock. Or plummeted so deep into the pool of water he wouldn't be able to make it to the surface for another breath. Especially if the water took over, rushing and spinning him, pulling him deep in its depths.

No!

She dragged her focus up from that murky pool, up to the top of the falls. But the sight there ripped a scream from her throat. Standing on a tree protruding from the bank out over the water was a figure. Two figures. Holding hands.

And the smaller had that shock of black hair she would recognize anywhere.

A SCREAM RIPPED through Caleb's thoughts, and he jerked upright as his heart nearly leapt from his chest.

His gaze swept around him, trying to find the source of the sound. Its terror still hammered through him.

The waterfall thundered nearby, pulling his focus that way. The base where the cascading liquid struck the pool. Up higher. The overhang.

His heart surged into his throat. There at the top, a tree hung over the river. Two figures stood on the log, and he'd know River Boy anywhere.

He lunged to his feet, ignoring the twinge from his ankle. He might regret this later, his ankle would for sure. But for now, fear carried him as he leapt up the bank.

He ended up on all fours in the grass above, and when he pushed up to standing, his ankle buckled.

So he dropped back to his hands and knees, covering

ground like a bear as he charged up the hill toward the top of the falls. If only he could run as fast as a grizzly in this position.

The climb seemed to take hours, and the roar of the falls drowned out every other sound. At last, he neared the top. The fallen tree was a cedar, with a massive root system and hundreds of tiny branches spreading out from the trunk. The thing must have been dead a year or so, for all the needles had fallen off. The fingerlike branches were brittle and sharp enough to be porcupine quills.

The tree had fallen through a section of dense underbrush, which meant the easiest way to reach the river would be to crawl along the prickly trunk.

He had to reach those two children before one of them slipped and tumbled over the edge of the falls.

As he climbed up on the thick log, the rough bark bit into his hands. Once he found his balance on top, he caught sight of two heads at the other end of the tree.

He started to call out for the boy, but a thought clamped a hand over his mouth. If he distracted them, would they lose their balance?

Maybe. He couldn't risk it.

Crawling forward on his hands and knees, he started through the massive branches. They were too thick for him to weave between each spiking limb. He had to charge forward over the top of them. Spears pricked his hands and body as he traveled, leaving his palms bloody. A few branches slapped his face when he removed his weight from them.

But he never took his eyes off the children ahead. About two horse lengths separated him from them now, and he kept himself focused on that last bit of distance he had to cover.

Pop-pank was talking to River Boy, motioning down over the ledge of the falls.

He wanted to shout, *No! Don't point down or your balance*

might sway that direction. And the way she clutched River Boy's hand, she would carry the boy with her.

God, no! Save them. Please.

What would Otskai do if she lost her son? He couldn't imagine the devastation. Couldn't imagine losing the boy who'd grown so firmly in Caleb's own heart. They couldn't lose him.

River Boy saw him and turned with a grin wide enough to brighten the darkest night. His mouth moved, but Caleb couldn't understand the words smothered by the roar of water.

He paused long enough to raise a hand toward the boy. "Stay there! Don't move."

Maybe River Boy thought he was calling him, extending a hand for the boy to come. The lad let go of his cousin and took a step toward Caleb.

His toddling gate was never very steady, and much less so now as he balanced on the skinny tip of the tree. As he took his second step, his foot slipped off the side of the trunk.

The boy's expression shifted from pure joy to sheer panic—a sight Caleb would remember as long as he lived.

River Boy's arms flailed in wild circles as he teetered sideways. Pop-pank screamed and grabbed for him, latching onto his shoulder as he tumbled.

The effort stole her own balance, and she pitched headfirst into the icy flow.

CHAPTER 23

Otskai sprinted toward the base of the falls, but no matter how fast she ran, her legs moved impossibly slow. When the two small forms at the top of the falls fell from the log, her heart ceased beating completely. Her lungs wouldn't draw breath.

God in heaven. Save my son. I beg You. Please.

Everything in her hoped Caleb had been speaking truth when he said his God cared about them all. Only a God powerful enough to create the world could save her son now.

She was near the base of the falls and slowed to scan the cascading water once more. She couldn't see the water in the river above to know for sure whether they'd tumbled over the falls or not. Should she check the pool at the base of the falls to see if they were caught under water? Or go around to the top of the falls to try to save them from falling over? Either way she might waste precious minutes that meant the difference between life and death for her baby.

In that second of indecision, something dark appeared at the top of the falls. As the spot tipped over the ledge and dropped with the cascading water, another scream wrenched from her throat.

Her son!

She half-slipped down the steep bank, but before she could charge into the water, another figure appeared at the edge of her gaze, tumbling down the falls.

Pop-pank. And a half second later...a man?

As the larger body writhed in midair, twisting for a better position to hit the water below, her heart seized even more.

Caleb. How had he come here? How had he found the children?

Yet as much as she feared for his safety, part of her terror eased with the knowledge of his presence. Caleb was an excellent swimmer. He could help. If her son survived the fall, Caleb would save him.

She couldn't rely on that hope. She had to act too. Both children needed help.

She refocused on the water's surface, straining to find the children. Did the clutches of this river still hold them both in its depths? And Caleb too. How deep was this cauldron?

She couldn't waste time. Every half second mattered. She charged into the water toward the place she'd seen her son land. Pop-pank had also splashed below the surface near that spot.

After a few steps in, the water was almost to her waist. The pressure against her forced her to slow. The swift current was already dragging her sideways.

Then a new thought slammed in. If the press of the river was pulling her so hard that she had to fight against it, the current would carry tiny bodies so much easier.

She shifted her angle to where the children might be now and bent low to move faster.

A splash ahead lifted her focus, and her heart leapt as a head with long black braids cleared the surface.

Pop-pank.

Otskai surged forward, using her hands to push the water behind her. In her long-ago childhood, before that awful day when the river swallowed both of her parents, her father had taught her to swim. He'd been an excellent swimmer, which was how she knew that raging river had been every bit as bad as she remembered—as awful as what she'd relived in so many nightmares. Churning, foaming water that could wrench the lives of both her parents was a force to fear indeed.

A force she now had to face.

The girl thrashed a little downriver from her, the current carrying her away even as she fought to swim against it.

Otskai honed every bit of her strength into forcing her way through the water toward the girl. She was up to her neck and would need to swim soon. Maybe she could push off with her feet to cover the last few arm lengths to the child. Then somehow, she'd find a way to swim them back to shore.

Surely, she could.

Her heart cried out to find her son. And Caleb. Why hadn't they surfaced? Were they stuck somewhere in the deep water, tangled by branches or rocks? In need of her help?

Searching for them could take precious seconds and still be fruitless. And she had a definite chance to save Pop-pank. With every breath, every heartbeat, the river current was pulling the girl farther from her. If she didn't act now, this life she had the chance to save could be lost. She couldn't let that happen.

Coiling her body, she pushed off from the river bottom and surged forward as hard as she could.

She covered half the distance to the girl, not as much as she'd been hoping for.

But she'd seen Caleb and others swim with powerful strokes through the water. She could do this.

Leading with her right hand, she reached forward and

pushed a handful of water behind her. Her body didn't stay high in the water like others did. She reached with the other hand, making up some of the distance. The current helped, carrying her along as it was doing with Pop-pank.

She moved the first arm again, then the second. Her nose clogged with water, choking her, burning her throat. But she ignored it.

Stroke after stroke, at last her fingers brushed the girl's sleeve. *Please, God.* With the other hand, she reached farther and gripped the first thing she touched. A slender arm.

Her heart leapt, and she clutched tight to Pop-pank's arm. Now she had to get them to shore, which would require more swimming. Her feet couldn't touch bottom here.

Pop-pank turned in the water and grabbed onto Otskai's arm, then gripped her shoulder, working her way up until the girl finally clung tight to her neck.

As much as she wanted to stop and hold the child, reassure her they would be safe, Pop-pank's clutch was pushing them both down into the water.

"No." She held the girl tight around the waist and tried to lay her body sideways in the water to spread their weight. Maybe this way they wouldn't sink as quickly.

A sound from behind—a man's voice—broke through her panic. Otskai twisted, throwing them off balance once more. But she had to see if that was Caleb. Was he safe? Had he found River Boy?

Someone was splashing in the water near the falls. How had the current not carried them downriver too?

She caught sight of a strong set of shoulders, a head of dark brown hair she'd seen plastered with water more than once.

And was that...? A mound of solid black in front of Caleb was all she caught sight of before a wave splashed hard in her face.

She coughed and sputtered, twisting again to put herself and the girl in a better position. That had to be her son in front of Caleb. If he had River Boy, both would be safe.

It seemed to take forever to get herself and Pop-pank closer to the edge of the river. She finally gave way to the current and let it carry them as she struggled toward the bank.

But ahead, a boulder loomed in their path.

She took in a breath of clear air and tried to silence the panic welling. Water foamed around the rock in an angry froth. Yet this stone could be their safety if she maneuvered right.

Drawing the child up in front of her, she pushed her legs forward to meet the rock first. Her feet struck the stone, and the shock of the blow reverberated through her lower half. But she held firm, letting the water push her and the girl up against the stony surface.

She could finally catch her breath and make a plan for how to get them the last of the distance to the shore. If she were a strong swimmer, she might be able to manage it in three or four good strokes. At least to the place where she could stand on solid ground.

But she wasn't a strong swimmer, especially when she had only one hand to work with and a heavy child clinging to her neck.

There were a few smaller rocks near this one. Maybe she could catch hold of those. But she'd have to be careful the current didn't throw them too hard against the stones. Then maybe one more solid kick away from those rocks would get her to shallower water.

A whimper by her ear dropped her focus to the girl, who'd pressed her face to Otskai's shoulder.

She wrapped both arms around Pop-pank and gave her a gentle squeeze. "We're all right." She didn't know enough Shoshone words to say more, at least with her mind so addled.

But pulling the girl into a hug probably helped as much as words did. She sent a glance up at the bank. Where was Watkeuse? She must still be at the village searching. Or maybe she'd recruited others to help look. Did she even know the children had climbed to the top of the falls? Maybe not.

The thought tightened Otskai's throat again. She couldn't expect help then. She'd have to get them to shore herself.

With God's help.

The thought pressed hard. Yes, He'd kept these three alive even after they'd plummeted over the edge of the falls and spent so long underwater.

She cast her gaze upriver to find Caleb and her son. No heads bobbed in the water. No splashing. Caleb must have already swum out with the boy. He probably lay on solid ground now, recovering. She well knew that feeling. That utter weakness that came after facing death in the eye.

But she couldn't lose strength yet. Refocusing on the next rocks she had to reach, she tightened her body and prepared to launch toward them.

The moments of rest had helped, for she had enough strength to reach the stones. They dug into her hip as the water surged around her, pressing her against them.

But Otskai focused on the next section of water. If she could get enough momentum, she might reach the shallows without having to swim. Or maybe only a stroke or two.

Give me the strength, God. Please. When this was over, she had a great many questions for Caleb. This God who would come through for her in the darkest of times, she wanted to know more of Him. Everything about Him. He'd proved He could be trusted, even when she didn't expect Him to do what she asked.

With the fresh strength lightening her, she crouched against the rocks, then pushed hard to surge forward with the girl.

Three strokes later, her foot struck ground. Her baby toe

actually, but the pain brought only pleasure. She scrambled for a better hold on the slippery rocks beneath her feet.

When she could finally straighten, she pressed forward. She couldn't stop until they were both on the bank. She'd make sure Pop-pank wasn't hurt, then find her son and the man she loved.

The man she loved.

Yes, she loved Caleb, no matter how she'd tried to ignore it before. And somehow, she would find a way to open herself to the possibility of a life with him.

At last, she took the final step onto dry ground and dropped to her knees, leaning forward until she could lay Pop-pank on the grass. The girl still clung to her, and Otskai rested her cheek against the child's. "We're safe."

The girl was shivering. For that matter, Otskai was too. But she had to get to her son and Caleb.

Easing the child's hands away from her neck, Otskai rose up to sit on her heels. Pop-pank's frightened eyes stared back at her, and Otskai held the girl's hands. She struggled to find the right Shoshone words. "I need to help the others. Can you come? Or rest here?"

Pop-pank looked dazed at first, but then understanding flashed in her gaze, and she scrambled up to sitting. She rattled off something Otskai couldn't decipher, but she seemed intent on going with her.

Otskai pushed to her feet and helped the child stand, then turned upriver. As they started on shaky legs, they helped each other stay upright.

She scanned the bank ahead. Patches of brush and low trees clustered in some areas, and the ground grew steep near the base of the falls. She couldn't see Caleb or her son anywhere, but they were probably down the embankment.

She broke into a run, new worries strengthening her legs with every step. With Caleb's broken ankle, he wouldn't be able to walk on his own. That was probably why they'd stayed at the edge of the river. Was there something else wrong with either of them? Had River Boy hit his head? Had Caleb's injury kept him from getting them to safety?

She kept her eyes focused on the land ahead, especially the top of the bank near the falls. But then a motion at the corner of her gaze caught her attention.

She slid a look toward the spot, and her mind struggled to register the sight. Out in the water, in the middle of the river, something floated. Something large and brown. Like...a man, floating face down. Caleb? But where was her son?

Then a splash came at one side, and a black head bobbed above the surface.

River Boy! Her son slapped at the water, panic flailing his arms.

Her heart pounded, and she lunged to the bank nearest them. What had happened to Caleb? He'd been well just minutes before.

She barely stopped herself before plunging out into the water. Caleb and her son were flowing freely down the river, which meant she had to strike out farther downstream to have any hope of catching them.

God, where are you? Had it really been Him who helped her reach Pop-pank and get the girl to shore? It had to have. There was no way Otskai could have swam through that water on her own.

So why wasn't He saving Caleb and her boy?

She sprinted downstream to a place that looked about right, awareness sinking over her. This was the place she and Pop-pank had crawled out of the water. She could use these rocks to push herself out and catch Caleb.

She didn't waste time, just charged out into the river. Sludging through the force of the flow was becoming too familiar. When she reached water deep enough to cover her chest, she pushed off from the river bottom and swam as hard as she could to reach the first group of rocks. She paused only long enough to glance at Caleb and River Boy.

The lad was using Caleb to keep him afloat and had turned Caleb's body on his back. Caleb looked so pale against the water's dark surface.

As pale as death.

CHAPTER 24

No! Otskai wanted to scream but kept the sound in. She needed all her breath.

And Caleb couldn't be dead. *God, no! Just when You brought us together. Just when I finally realized how silly my selfish need for independence was. Don't take him away. You can't take him away.*

Maybe a God powerful enough to create the world and every one of the people in it could raise Caleb back to life. *Revive him, Almighty God. He's surely one of Your best creations.*

She kicked off from the rocks and braced herself for the current to slam her against the larger boulder. The blow took her breath, but she fought to focus on the next step.

Caleb and her son were coming quickly. They would float near enough that she could push off from this rock and grab ahold of them. Probably. But how would she drag them both to shore?

Somehow, Caleb's body hadn't sunk into the murky depths of the hungry water. That must be God's doing, for his body was keeping her son afloat.

He'd given his life for her boy. The thought nearly doubled

her over with pain. She blinked against the sting of tears and fought to push the notion away.

Bring him back to life, God. Please. And help me get them to shore.

She gathered herself, keeping her gaze on the two floating bodies. River Boy caught sight of her and reached out with his free hand. His "Mama! Mama!" ripped at her heart.

But she couldn't let emotions knock aside the focus she needed for this next effort.

When they'd nearly reached her, she kicked off from the rock, launching into the powerful current. She'd calculated correctly the speed Caleb and River Boy were floating, but she'd misjudged the pressure the water would push on her.

After two strong strokes, though, her hand caught hold of Caleb's upper arm. River Boy clung to his other side and began to climb over Caleb to reach her. That shift in weight pressed Caleb down under the water.

Panic surged through Otskai, and she reached over Caleb to still her son, grasping his arm and pushing him back. "I'm here, son. Be still. We have to swim to shore."

The boy probably didn't understand her words, especially with his own panic clouding his mind. But he clung with both hands to the arm she had draped over Caleb, which took his weight off the man.

She'd been kicking her legs and using the current to help stay afloat without adding her own weight to Caleb.

But with her son clinging tight to her arm that was draped across Caleb, that didn't leave her much to use for swimming.

Still, if she maneuvered, she would have one free arm and both legs. Maybe there would be a rock along the way she could use to brace their flow.

A glance downriver showed nothing close. There was one pointed rock a distance down that looked as if it might do more harm than good. And it was so far downriver. If Caleb didn't get out of this water before then, even God may not be able to bring him back to life.

Get us out of the water before then, God. Please. Bring him back.

She swam with everything she had toward the bank. Her arms and legs had possessed no more strength when she and Pop-pank had crawled from the river. At least that was what she'd thought. Yet now, they seemed stronger than ever before as she kicked and paddled through the water.

Were they making any headway? The river seemed better able to move them along then she was. Maybe if she angled diagonally instead of trying to swim straight to the bank, she could harness the power of the flow.

That seemed to make a difference. She kicked and paddled and kicked and paddled. Soaking in breaths when she could manage them. The need for air became more vital, and she slowed enough to draw in a few deeper breaths.

But what of Caleb's need for air? A glance back at him and his lifeless face tightened the panic in her chest again. His lips were parted, but she couldn't be still enough to know if he was breathing.

How *could* he be breathing after spending so much time face down in the water? How long had he been like that? She had no idea.

Why wasn't he coming back to life?

She renewed her focus on reaching the shore. *Bring him back to life, God. Please.*

She'd covered about half the distance to the bank, still moving diagonally to let the water's flow help her. She didn't stop swimming, but cast a glance downriver to the pointed rock.

It was so much closer. At this rate, they would have drifted well past it before she finally got them to shore. Though the stone had only been an internal measure, her failure churned another rise of panic through her. Her chest was nearly to bursting, and her throat tightened so much she could barely draw breath.

She *needed* breath for every stroke and kick.

God, get us there. Bring Caleb back to life.

Exhaustion seeped through her limbs, and her body screamed for air. She gasped in another breath even as her legs slowed their kicking.

She had to keep going. Had to summon the strength. Caleb and her son needed her to do this.

God, please! If you love any of us. Any of these creations Caleb says mean so much to you. Please. Save us. All three of us.

A wave surged over them, splashing the side of her face, spraying water up her nose and down her throat. Her body reacted without her consent, coughing and hacking to rid itself of the dirty spray. The convulsions stole the last of her breath and energy.

Her arms went limp, and she was powerless to refill their strength. Her legs gave only feeble kicks, and another wave crashed over them.

But as her face dipped into the water, a woman's cry met her ears.

"My sister!"

That voice. She would know it anywhere. Watkeuse.

Maybe God truly had sent help.

EVERY PART OF CALEB ACHED. *Ached* was such a puny word for the agony inside him, but his mind hurt too much to think of worse.

He lay still, letting his eyes stay closed as he worked out what was happening around him.

He must be lying on the grass. Was he still on the river's bank soaking his leg in the water? His ankle felt like someone had swung an ax into it. People were nearby. Their voices drifted around him.

A flash of memory slipped in. He'd been running up the side of the falls on all fours. That was why his ankle hurt so much. He might've rebroken the bone.

But why had he been running?

The next memory came slow and murky, just like the water he'd been swimming through. Searching for the children. Panic welled inside him, tensing his entire body as he struggled to recall whether he'd found the little ones.

River Boy. He'd searched the muddy depths until he located the lad and freed him from the branch holding him underwater. They'd made it to the surface. He'd been swimming them to shore. The boy had yelled something, and Caleb turned to look at him. Then...

The pain at the base of his skull pounded even harder. He must've hit his head on a rock. He didn't remember it, but that seemed the only likely scenario.

Now, voices were buzzing around him. Languages he couldn't understand, at least not without a lot of thought. And even easy thoughts brought pain.

Something cool and soft touched his temple, then stroked down his cheek. A hand.

Then one voice called to him above all the others. "My love."

Otskai.

Her words wove through him. She spoke English, the language he actually could understand. But with her sweet lilting accent, the sound slipped through him, infusing him with strength.

Enough strength to open his eyes.

She was there, her beautiful face studying him. The worry in her eyes tightened his chest.

He opened his mouth to tell her he was fine, to erase that worry. But parting his lips was a harder task than he'd expected.

His mouth seemed glued shut. He forced his tongue in between his lips, ran it over the bottom one for moisture. Then tried to speak again.

But as he was about to say he was all right, a new thought pressed in. River Boy. He'd left the lad in the water, though he certainly hadn't meant to. Maybe her worry was for her son. Had he…had they…lost him?

That was the name that slipped from his lips. "River Boy?"

Otskai's gaze softened, and she looked over at something beside her. When she motioned, another figure moved close.

That sweet face so much like his mother's smiled down at Caleb, his pudgy cheeks dimpling. "Caleb."

Relief and joy swept through him. He would never tire of hearing the boy say his name in that cute little voice.

Caleb lifted a hand and laid it on the boy's leg. Movement was getting a little easier. He gave the lad a squeeze. "Hey there, son. Looks like you made out better than I did." His voice rasped, and his throat burned as if he'd swallowed fire. But at least his body seemed to be working again.

Otskai laid a gentle hand on his forearm, and Caleb shifted his gaze to her. He turned his hand to slide her palm into his.

Her eyes glistened as she closed her fingers around his. "Thank you for saving him. You are hurt very much."

He almost shook his head but paused just in time to save himself from a new pounding. He'd been at this invalid stuff long enough to know better.

Instead, he gave her a smile. "No. Not much more than before, just my ankle."

Her brows lowered in worry. With her free hand, she reached up toward his head.

At first, he thought she might stroke his cheek as she had before, but then her fingers slipped around to the back of his skull. The moment she touched the tender spot, fire flared inside him, bringing enough heat to start him sweating. He fought to conceal his reaction, but she must have seen him flinch.

She jerked her hand back, the horror on her face quickly slipping into an expression that looked close to tears.

He worked for a smile. Worked hard for it. But he had to show her she'd not made things worse. "I'm all right."

Her gaze proved he hadn't convinced her. So he reached for the hand she'd jerked back.

She seemed hesitant to meet his reach, but then she let him take her hand. Now he held both of hers. But this one, he eased closer to himself, close enough to press a kiss on her palm.

Her eyes drifted shut, clearing away the fear from moments before. He pressed another kiss, then brushed her palm over his cheek. He was so rough these days, his stubble might be uncomfortable for her. But he needed this connection, and he suspected she did as well.

At last, she opened her eyes. The love there nearly melted him.

He stroked his thumb across the back of her hand. If there weren't so many people around, he would sit up and pull her into an embrace, then kiss her soundly. The real kind that showed her how much she meant to him.

But River Boy squirmed, breaking the moment of connection. Otskai pulled her hands away to adjust her son. This was a good time for Caleb to sit up too.

He pressed his palms to the ground and started to ease upright, but the world around him spun as light flashed through his vision.

"Ho, there. Don't think you're ready to get up just yet." Susanna's voice sounded from behind him, and her tone brooked no opposition.

Caleb laid his head back on the ground, letting his eyes drop shut. He took in long, deep breaths as his head began to settle. Whatever whacked his skull had done a job on him. Maybe a few more minutes of rest would repair him enough to try rising again.

As if she'd heard his thoughts, Susanna's voice came again. "You just settle yourself in, Caleb Jackson. You're going to rest until your body says it's ready to get up."

Caleb had to bite back a response. As much as he respected Susanna, he'd get up when he wanted to. His body would have to do what he told it.

But when he opened his eyes, his gaze found Otskai. The love from moments before was still there but clouded by worry. For him.

He reached for her hand again and stroked his thumb across the back of smooth skin. For this woman, he would do just about anything. Even be still.

CHAPTER 25

Otskai sat beside the river, staring into the calm pool where she'd washed clothes with Watkeuse only the day before. So much had happened since then. It seemed a lifetime ago.

God had brought them through. She had no doubt His hand had been the one to carry her and Pop-pank through the water to reach the shore. Even now, when she lifted her gaze to the swift current farther out, fear tingled through her. But God had given her the strength necessary.

And He brought Caleb back to life. She glanced at the man beside her, his strong profile staring out at the same river as he soaked his injured ankle in the cold water. He must've felt her look, for he glanced at her with one of his smiles that made her belly flip.

His gaze lingered on her, making her want to scoot closer. Into the crook of his arm, near enough for him to kiss her. Heat flared up her neck at the thought.

But before she could jerk her gaze away, he reached out his hand, laying it palm up on the ground between them.

She placed her hand in his, relishing his warmth, the rough

callouses that came from a life lived in earnest. His thumb caressed her knuckles, and she closed her fingers a little tighter around his. She would never tire of this connection between them.

Behind them both, her son stirred on the fur pallet she'd laid in the grass. He'd slept more than once today, probably still recovering from yesterday's excitement.

She glanced back at the boy to see if he was waking, and Caleb did the same.

River Boy's eyes were still closed, his face serene in complete relaxation. So innocent.

Caleb gave her a gentle squeeze, drawing her focus back to him. "He went through a lot yesterday. It's a miracle he came away with nothing worse than exhaustion." He'd been speaking English since they came out of the river. His head probably needed time to recover before he again tasked his mind with speaking in a new language.

Emotion rose up to burn Otskai's throat as she held Caleb's gaze. "A very big miracle."

Elan had taught her that word yesterday as they talked through the events. *Something that seems impossible yet actually happened. An act only God could do.* That's exactly what had happened in this river.

Her eyes burned as the memory rose of Caleb lying face-down in the water. "A miracle that you're alive. When I saw you floating with your face in the water, I thought you were dead."

He squinted, his gaze lifting above her into the distance. "I don't know exactly what happened. I believe God has the power to do anything. Whether that means finding a way to get me air just in time. Or bringing me back to life."

Exactly as she'd prayed. *Thank you, God.*

Caleb's dark eyes showed that his mind was working on something. She could watch those eyes for days and still be fascinated by them. They revealed so much of his heart. His goodness. His struggles.

But when he spoke, the words weren't at all what she'd expected.

"Will you tell me what happened? In a river. What first made you fear the water?"

Her mind instantly knew what he was speaking of. Not yesterday. Not any of the other river crossings where he'd had to save her life. That first time.

"If you can. Or if you'd rather not..." His eyes showed a gentleness, the compassion that was part of what she loved about him.

She would rather *not* relive that story, but if she was going to open herself fully to Caleb, that was where it all started. She moistened her lips as she brought up the memories. Where to begin?

Maybe at the most important part. She let her gaze wander toward the calm pool as she found the right words. "My parents were wonderful. I remember our home being happy. Full of joy and love.

"Our camp was in a different place when I was young, but still beside a river. A wide river near the mountains. When the snow melted, the water flowed fast, rising over the banks."

She didn't let herself linger on the image that flashed with those words, just pushed on. "My father taught me to swim. The three of us would go to the river and play. I only have small memories of that, but I remember how strong my father was. How far each stroke carried him through the water."

She would love to live in those happy memories longer, but she had to keep going. "One time when I was seven winters old, the water ran faster. Angry. Churning and foaming at the rocks. I swam too far, and I remember hearing their calls. But I couldn't get back, the water was carrying me too fast."

She worked to keep her breathing steady. Not to lose herself in the memory. "There was no one else with us. I was fighting to get to shore, but the water kept pulling me under. I hit rocks that spun me and flipped me into the dark below. I couldn't breathe.

"At last, my father grabbed me. He pulled me through the water as he swam toward the shore. We were almost there, then he let go." Tears surged as that moment of panic welled through her again.

"I didn't know what happened, but I was close enough to reach the shore on my own. Maybe he knew that and went back for my mother. But by the time I pulled myself out and looked back, they were both gone.

"My aunt heard our screams and found me running along the bank, calling for my parents. I never found them, but one of the braves saw my mother's body later. Much farther downriver."

She took a moment to steady her breathing. To pull herself from those images. The rest shouldn't be so hard.

At last, she glanced at Caleb to see his reaction. He'd been so quiet. And maybe he knew that would help her get the story out.

But the moment she saw the red rimming his eyes, the tears glistening there, a fresh wave of love for this man swept through her. He squeezed her hand but didn't say anything. Yet that touch was enough to strengthen her for the rest of her tale.

"I lived with my aunt and uncle after that. And Watkeuse and her four older brothers." She raised her brows, letting that last detail speak for itself.

The corners of Caleb's mouth tipped up, brightening the tears still glistening in his eyes. "No wonder you learned to fight for yourself."

A chuckle slipped out, too loud with the chaos of her emotions. "Watkeuse taught me that more than anyone."

The smile stayed in Caleb's eyes even when his mouth sobered. His silence gave her freedom to press on once more.

"A few moons after I came to live with them, my uncle formed the contract for me to marry Motsqueh."

All hint of pleasure fled Caleb's expression, and his hand tightened around hers. Not painful, but nothing soft remained. "How old were you?" The question came out in a growl, laced with more anger than she'd seen from him.

She'd better clarify things before she loosed a bear. "It was only a contract, to be fulfilled when I came of age. I was eight winters old when the agreement was made."

Caleb was breathing now, and not quite so rigid, but anger still rose from him. He seemed to be working to control it. "How did you feel about it?"

She honed her gaze on his face, trying to decipher what he wanted to know specifically. His eyes seem to be searching deep inside her. As if he really cared what her thoughts had been about being promised to a brave at such a young age. She'd not had the option to refuse the contract. No one had ever asked her opinion. No one save Watkeuse, and she'd been a young girl too. But Caleb wanted to know, even all these years after it no longer mattered.

She struggled to form her thoughts into words, English words at that. "It...frightened me. He was twelve summers older than me. A man, when I was only a girl. I didn't know him. Maybe if I'd come to know him in the years before we were wed, it would've been different. But we lived in separate worlds."

Caleb's brows lowered, in thought probably, for the anger no longer seemed to pulse through him. "You didn't have that chance before your marriage?"

Heat swept through Otskai, as though she was still that half-grown girl watching across the camp as the braves rode out for the hunt. She shook her head. "He was one of the warriors. I was only a girl."

Caleb shook his head, and with his brow still furrowed, he

didn't seem happy with her answer. "And your marriage with him? Was he good to you?" Then he blinked, and red splotched his cheeks. "I mean...I'm not asking..."

He paused to take in a breath. "I guess I want to know... well... I really want to know, were you happy with him? Was he kind to you?" His eyes searched hers, his earnestness melting any barrier she tried to build between them.

But still, she turned away from his gaze to collect her thoughts, staring into the calm pool in front of them. "I tried not to let myself think about being happy. He wasn't mean. Didn't strike me or force me to do things I couldn't. He provided food for us in the hunt and through trade." She wasn't answering the questions Caleb was really asking. But it felt wrong to speak ill of a man who hadn't ever hurt her, at least not intentionally.

She slid a glance at Caleb to see if he would settle for the answer she'd given. He was watching her. Waiting for more. Giving her time, but still waiting.

She faced the water again. "He wasn't cruel, but he was hard to please. I think all husbands must be. It took me a while to learn how to do things the way he wanted. When he was gone, I could cook as I wished, work my camas fields, care for our home in ways that brought me happiness. When he came back, my focus had to be on what made him happy."

As she spoke the words, their selfishness clanged in her ears. Wasn't that a woman's role, to care for her husband's needs? And she was complaining about it? Caleb would see her true faults now.

She tried for a casual shrug. "It's the way of a man and woman who are married. I just...wasn't prepared for it, I suppose."

Caleb tugged her hand enough to bring her focus back to him. Then he leaned in, his eyes more intense than usual "Otskai, the way of a man and woman when they're joined in marriage before God is to commit themselves to help the other. To love, care for, and respect the other. The Bible says a man should love his wife as he loves himself."

He eased back, as though trying to slow his passion. "I didn't know Motsqueh, and I didn't see how things were between you. But I do know that when God blesses a union of like minds and hearts, when a man and woman are joined together in service to Him and to each other—each serving the other—the marriage is strong and founded in love and joy and unity."

She didn't know the word *unity*, but the thought of a shared love that brought joy raised a burn all the way up her throat to sear her eyes. Could that ever be possible for her?

She could imagine such a life with Caleb. But would it last? If she'd had such a thing with Motsqueh, how would life have been different?

One tear slipped past her defenses, and Caleb lifted a thumb to wipe it away. He didn't speak though, giving her space to share when she was ready.

And she needed to tell him this. More than anything, she wanted him to know this thing that *she* was only now realizing.

Another tear slipped down, even as she opened her mouth to speak. "Motsqueh was killed in a fight against a Crow war party. When my uncle brought me the news, I mourned as a wife should. I was sad his life had been taken in that way."

She could barely face him as she spoke the next awful truth. "But a tiny part of me was relieved. Even though I would give birth to a child without him, I was finally free to live my own life. I no longer had to submit to my uncle's whims. I no longer had to spend every moment trying to guess the thoughts of my husband—a man who I felt like little more than a servant to—or make myself better to please him. I could live as I wanted.

"Things weren't easy, especially in the first days after River Boy was born. But my camas fields thrived. I could trade for what we needed. I studied the best places to lay my traps, and we had all the food and furs we could want, as well as extra to trade. I felt almost guilty for being so happy. I promised myself I would never give my freedom to another, at least not willingly."

Caleb's gaze softened, yet a hint of sadness slipped into his eyes. He reached up to thumb another tear from her cheek and kept his hand near to cradle her face. "That's why you ran from me after our kiss."

A fresh wave of emotion clogged her throat, and she nodded. This man knew her so well. He had the ability to see deep inside her. And she no longer wanted to stop him.

With his hand still on her face, he wiped away another tear. Then his gaze locked with hers. "Otskai, I will always be completely honest with you. And because of that, I need to tell you that I plan to ask you to marry me."

A flood of joy swept through her, a new rush of feeling she could barely contain.

But before she could speak, he squeezed her hand. "I'm not asking now, I'm simply preparing you. But what you need to know is that I would only want you to be the person you really are. I would never want you to feel forced to do anything for me. Whatever you did or didn't do, I would want it to be from love. Love for me, and love for the God we both serve."

A sadness shadowed his gaze, and he leaned back. "That's why I'm not asking you yet. It's important to me that the woman I marry also knows and loves my God. Maybe I shouldn't have said all this. I don't want anything between us to affect your decision about Him."

Laughter bubbled inside her. "I have so many questions to ask you about Him. But first, I need to tell you what happened." She shared about her desperate prayers the day before, how she'd known nothing could save Caleb except the God powerful enough to create the world. How she'd begged that God to bring him back to life.

Caleb's mouth curved as she spoke, but it was the sparkle in his eyes that lit his entire face. When she finished speaking, he cradled her hand in both of his. "And He did. He carried us all through and kept us all safe. He answered your prayers."

She nodded, a fresh stream of tears slipping down her cheeks. She'd stopped trying to hold them back, which meant she would be a blubbery mess soon. It would be a test of Caleb's words about wanting her as she truly was.

A giggle slipped out at the thought. She was such a jumble of emotions, crying and laughing all at once.

Caleb tipped his head, his smile turning curious. "What's funny?"

She shook her head. "I'm just happy." She placed her other hand on his, so all four of their hands were joined. "You make me happy."

The laughter in Caleb's eyes deepened into a different kind of intensity, and he pulled one of his hands from hers and lifted it again to her cheek. "I feel just the same." His voice held a rich depth that rumbled through her, stirring a delicious tingle.

His hand slipped around her neck, drawing her closer. His eyes dipped to her lips, and that was the last thing she saw before her own eyelids slipped closed.

His taste was even more delicious than she remembered. His mouth both gentle and intense. She relished the strength of him. He'd always made her feel so steady, so safe. But this kiss...it swept her off her feet until she had to cling to him for balance. She pressed closer, breathing him in.

And then a tiny voice broke through her pleasure. "Mama?"

Otskai froze, squeezing her eyes against her disappointment. Of all the timing. She opened her eyes and pulled back from Caleb, sending him an apology with her gaze.

He looked as reluctant as she was.

Together, they turned to her son, who was sitting up on his fur pallet. His glossy black hair shone in the sunlight, and his eyes still held that sleepy squint. He rubbed a fist in one, then raised his gaze to her and Caleb. This time he looked between the two of them, really awake now.

She started to reach for him, but the boy's eyes caught on the man and brightened. "Caleb."

The joy lighting his face made that same emotion surge inside her again. How wonderful that they both loved this man so much.

Caleb reached out for her son, and River Boy scrambled forward. Caleb grabbed him under the arms and swung him upward and around, plopping him down in his lap with enough bounce to bring a giggle from the boy.

The grin on Caleb's face as he studied the lad held more than pleasure. If she wasn't mistaken, that was love shining from his eyes.

She leaned into Caleb's side, resting her head on his shoulder. He wrapped his arm around her waist and tugged her near.

She would happily stay in that place forever—snuggled beside the two boys she loved.

EPILOGUE

"So, three more days, eh?"

Joel's question made Caleb lift his focus from the adjustments he was making on his rifle. Over these last two weeks of rest, he'd done everything he could to keep his hands busy. Cleaning all their guns, sharpening knives, sanding pots, scraping hides. And now he'd returned his focus to an early task, adjusting the sights on his rifle as he sat with the other four men outside of camp.

He nodded to Joel. "Three more days and we can ride out. I can go about anywhere with the walking sticks now, and my ankle hasn't swollen in almost a week." Even Otskai had agreed his condition was improved enough for travel.

Heat slid through him as he thought of the kiss he'd rewarded her with after she gave her consent. Thankfully, River Boy was too young to notice their moments of affection even when he was nearby. A good thing, for Caleb planned many more moments like that for years to come. Until God saw fit to take Caleb to heaven—a place Otskai would eventually join him in. *Thank You, Lord.*

"I suspect it's more than the thought of long days in the

saddle that has you grinning ear to ear." Adam's voice tugged Caleb from those pleasant thoughts.

Yep, Adam was right. His cheeks kept a constant ache from all his smiles these days. But how could he not grin with Otskai nearby?

These fellows weren't worth the effort to wipe the pleasure from his face, but he did try to settle his smile a bit. He worked for an innocent tone as he raised his brows at Adam. "I just know how eager you are to get back that tomahawk for Meksem. You said you wouldn't marry her until you could give it to her, right?"

That reminder turned the others' focus on Adam—and off of Caleb.

Even with his Spanish coloring, Adam's ears turned red as his face found a grin of his own. And for once, Adam couldn't seem to find words to respond. Only a nod.

Thoughtful silence slipped through their group as they each worked on whatever project they'd brought or simply stared out toward the river in the distance. It had been a while since it was just the five of them, the men who'd started out on their original journey. They'd certainly found adventure along the way—far more than they'd ever expected.

After long moments, Joel's voice broke the quiet, his tone sober. "And what then? After you marry Meksem, where do we go next? Or do we all settle down like old men? Sit around our lodges with our women and babies and tell stories like the Gray Hairs?"

A huff slipped from Beaver Tail. Clearly not what he planned to do. But for Caleb's part, that picture sounded pretty close to heaven.

Really, any image that included Otskai and River Boy sounded perfect. But he had the lad to consider now. It would be hard for the boy to keep traipsing off on adventures.

"You trying to tell us Elan's in the family way?" Adam's question brought Caleb around. The man was eyeing his brother with raised brows and something of a challenge in his smiling eyes.

Joel shook his head. "Not me. Not that I know of anyway. I was talking about Beaver's and Caleb's little ones."

As all four pairs of eyes honed in on him, heat flooded Caleb's face. His own ears were likely tomato red. He shook his head. "He's not mine yet."

But they all knew he planned to become River Boy's father soon. To raise the boy as his own.

These last two weeks had given him and Otskai time to speak of their life together. To dream of the future, to speak of hopes and plans. He didn't know exactly how their life would look yet. God hadn't pressed into his spirit what his next move should be.

But they were praying about it, both together and in their own private moments spent with the Lord. However the Father guided them, he and Otskai and River Boy would be a family, starting one day very soon.

A noise from the man at the end of their group pulled Caleb's focus from his thoughts.

Or maybe it was the lack of noise from French. The fellow had been quieter than usual these last few days. And now that Caleb thought about it, French hadn't said a word since they'd sat down out here at the edge of the camp.

He was staring off to the side, toward a line of trees. Caleb could only see his profile, but there was no pleasure in the outline. None of the jovial nature that had always been a trademark of French's personality.

Caleb leaned forward to better see the man around Joel and Adam. "What're you thinking about, French?"

His friend was slow to turn toward him, and when he did, his eyes didn't hold the smile his mouth tried to form. "Not much."

"This would normally be the time you'd tell us about the summer you spent trapping in a land so cold the rivers froze all year round. Or maybe the antelope you tamed so well you could ride it." Adam's joking words did bring a bit of a smile to French's eyes, but not the good-humored glimmer that usually lived there.

Instead, he shook his head. "I've never ridden an antelope. There was a buffalo one time, but that's a tale for another day."

Adam chuckled and clapped a hand on their friend's shoulder. "You're a good man, French. You amaze me. Every time."

French offered another grin before he turned his focus back toward those distant trees. His face sobered, and his eyes took on a wistfulness, as though he was longing for something far away.

No matter how many stories French told about his past, there always seemed to be so much he didn't say. What of his family? The friends he'd left behind? Had there been a woman? Surely not, as young as French had been when he started trapping on his own.

But something held the man a little separate from everyone around him. Maybe on the journey back through the mountains, Caleb could spend extra time with this man who'd become both brother and friend. Sometimes, a listening ear could help a person sort through his thoughts.

A motion near the river drew Caleb's attention, and the figures coming their way sent a smile through him. The women had taken River Boy and Pop-pank to look for berries in the brush by the water's edge.

His hungry gaze found Otskai, stepping away from the others as she chased after River Boy. His giggle echoed through the air as he ran from her. She caught him up, and his laugh turned to breathless chortles as she tickled his belly.

Those two. His heart ached with the depth of his love for them.

If not for his ankle, he would go to them now. Wrap the pair in his arms and hold them close. Maybe squeeze another giggle from the boy.

But he rose to his feet and waited with the other men as the group joined them. Otskai stepped to his side, and he tucked his arm around her, drawing her close, where she fit so perfectly.

He usually tried not to embarrass her with too much affection in front of the others, but he couldn't help pressing a kiss to the top of her head and breathing in the sweet scent of her.

She raised her face to his, her beauty washing through him anew. *Lord, how did I ever deserve such a woman?*

His answer came in her smile. This woman was God's gift to him. A grace he could never earn. An outpouring of the Father's love.

And that made him love her all the more.

Did you enjoy Caleb and Otskai's story? I hope so!
Would you take a quick minute to leave a review where you purchased the book?
It doesn't have to be long. Just a sentence or two telling what you liked about the story!

To receive a free book and get updates when new Misty M. Beller books release, go to https://mistymbeller.com/freebook

And here's a peek at the next book in the series (French's story!), Faith in the Mountain Valley:

Chapter One

Spring, 1831
Clearwater River Valley, Future Idaho Territory

Someone was coming.

French tensed as his spotted mare perked her ears toward the trees ahead of them. He rode near the back of their group. A position that let him slip into anonymity for the most part, but from here he could keep an eye on the others. Step in and help where needed. Then ease back just as quickly, without his presence making much of a stir. Like whoever was approaching through those trees.

Beaver Tail, riding in the front, would meet the strangers head on, assess any danger, and deal with it accordingly. Behind Beaver Tail, his wife Susanna never strayed far—his better-looking shadow, one might say. Meksem, another warrior, would be nearby as well, with her future husband Adam at her side.

The others settled in between and around, with Joel and his wife Elan bringing up the rear, ever watchful.

French never had an exact job. He was the one who adapted. Stepped in to gather wood or help where needed. More often than not, he provided a story for entertainment when the rest of them needed a distraction.

Who knew his life would be so haphazard, without focus or any kind of real plan? But here he was, a man of all work, yet nothing to call his own.

Maybe if he'd been able to find Colette, all of this would be different. His entire world would be different. Happy. His purpose had always been to please her. Because a smile on her sweet face filled him up like an overflowing canteen.

The day he'd lost her, he'd lost his purpose.

He'd never been able to find her again, so here he sat. Riding with his friends along the edge of a cliff, watching a cluster of pines and cedars for who knew what to step through.

Movement caught his eye beyond the trees, and his senses spiked. Indians. Not really a surprise to see out here in the mountain wilderness, yet... These braves wore the markings of the Blackfoot tribe.

And the Blackfoot had a reputation as a bully among the southern tribes.

Not Beaver Tail though. He was Blackfoot, at least half so, though to look at him you'd never know his father had been English. But the man had nothing of bully in him. Which just showed you could never judge a person according to their nationality. Better to judge by each fellow's own actions. And be cautious.

In front of him, Caleb's big frame blocked the sight of the oncoming riders for a moment. But when the trail shifted again, the strangers had multiplied to six now. The five in front were definitely Indian, probably Blackfoot. But the man in the back appeared white, although the slouch hat he wore made it hard to see more than pale skin. The man was lean, wiry even, but it was hard to tell more than that under his buckskins.

French's pulse picked up pace. A Frenchman maybe? The few trappers they'd met west of the Missouri had been part of the Hudson Bay Company, the sorry lot. And only half had spoken his native tongue, the rest being of British descent. A possibility more and more likely since that country had won ownership of the Canadian colonies.

But still, what he wouldn't give for another conversation in his mother language.

Beaver paused their group a few strides before the strangers. The high-low cadence of the Blackfoot tongue drifted on the breeze. French tried to focus on picking out words. He'd learned enough Blackfoot through the years to know they were asking where each was headed and what their business was. Friendly conversation, it sounded like. Good.

The word *Peigan* came clear. These five must be part of the more peaceful sect of the Blackfoot tribe. Maybe that would help ease any lingering concerns from the Nez Perce women in their group.

His gaze drifted to the white stranger in the rear, but his horse was positioned so the brave in front covered much of him. Only the pretty palomino the man rode could be seen plainly. The animal still wore its pale yellow winter coat, which would likely shed out in another month or two to produce a more golden or coppery color. But the lighter tone brought out the pale blonde of the man's hair, barely showing at his neck beneath the hat. Not many grown men could boast hair that light. A painful memory swept over him. Colette's father was the only other man he could recollect. Colette's hair had been even a shade lighter than her father's.

Movement where Beaver Tail was speaking pulled his

thoughts from Colette, thankfully. Even after all these years, she stayed too heartbreakingly close to the forefront of his mind.

Beaver Tail motioned farewell to the strangers. The path spanned wide enough for two to ride abreast, with a steep slope on one side and a sheer cliff dropping off on the other. Both parties would need to ride single file to pass. Good thing the oncoming riders appeared friendly.

As their group straggled out to pass in a single line, French readied the Blackfoot greeting on his tongue to offer as the men rode by. The lead brave appeared seasoned, at least fifty years old with plenty of salt worked through his long pepper braids.

French nodded and spoke the usual greeting. "*Oki*."

The brave gave an answering dip of his chin as he passed. One by one, each of the four other Blackfoot rode by him in quick succession, either offering a friendly nod or barely a notice.

As the last brave passed, French sent a hungry glance ahead to the white man bringing up the rear. Should he say *bonjour* or greet him in English?

The fellow gave no sign of his heritage. No word of greeting or even a smile. He wore his hat so low the brim covered most of his face. The fur collar of his coat pulled up to hide the point of his chin, which left only his mouth and the tip of his nose revealed. Those features were small, almost dainty for a man.

The fellow must be young. Maybe even a white captive they'd raised as a Blackfoot? But why then would he wear a white man's hat? So maybe not raised as a Blackfoot, but possibly still a captive?

"Hello." French spoke the word quietly, almost intimately. To show the lad he would find a friend in them if he needed one.

The fellow didn't lift his head to reveal his eyes. Didn't acknowledge French in any way until he'd almost passed by completely. Then he lifted a gloved hand from his reins in a little wave. A friendly greeting, no more.

But there was something in the motion. Something in those long, slender fingers that caught French's attention.

Those weren't the gloves a man wore. Not so well fitting. Nor was that the broad hand of a man. But more than that...the elegance of the movement stole his breath.

The rider had already passed, but French pulled his mare to a halt and spun in the saddle to watch the stranger. The outline was lean, definitely not a full-grown man. But a boy? The figure sat too tall. A lad of that height would be awkward and gangly. Not the poised elegance this person possessed.

It must be...a woman. Should he do something? She hadn't seemed afraid. Maybe she was married to one of the men. He'd seen trappers marry Indian women, the opposite was surely possible. Though white women in this wilderness were scarce.

Since she didn't appear in danger or desirous of help, maybe best to leave well enough alone.

∼

"You're awfully quiet tonight, French."

Caleb's words pulled French's gaze from the leaping flames of their campfire. The man had a way of seeing things a fellow tried to keep hidden. And a knack for making you want to confide in him.

During their years together, French had told him many stories from his eleven years of trapping, had even told Caleb that both his parents were dead. But that was the most he'd ever shared.

Not even Caleb's gentle steadiness could pull Colette from his lips. She was too important. And the rest...well, it was history. Another lifetime, and better left there.

So, he worked for a smile for his friend. "Just thinking about that group we met on the trail earlier." That was close enough to the truth. Seeing that white woman with the Blackfoot braves, trying to appear as a man, yet with hair almost as flaxen as Colette's had been, had resurrected too many childhood memories. The woman couldn't actually be Colette, not this far away from the Canadian fort her family had moved to. Yet the memories wouldn't stop.

He couldn't tell them to Caleb. Better to find another story.

"Reminded me of the time I spent with Jim Bridger and we passed by a group of Bloods and Gros Ventre. I'd never seen the two tribes travel together like that, nor have I since. But these fellows had spent the winter together and looked to be half starved." The rest of the group had shifted their focus to him and leaned in for the tale.

Maybe this really was his purpose in life, to entertain these friends. Maybe his eleven years on the trail had all been in preparation for this. First the nine years searching for Colette. Then the winter he'd spent desperately trying to forget her, and then this last year and a half with the men around him.

The women had joined on by ones or twos, mostly pairing up with his friends. Not that he begrudged Beaver Tail, Joel, Adam, and now Caleb happiness with their lady loves.

But once again, he was the odd man out.

He always would be, because he'd never settle for anyone but Colette. He'd promised her he wouldn't.

After he finished his story, Adam joined in with a tale of his own, one from when he traveled with the Mandan warriors on his way to find the Palouse horses. Adam had tried to get the rest of them to go with him, but when Joel—his younger brother—had put his foot down and said they'd finish their trek up the Missouri as planned, Adam had sneaked off in the middle of the night, leaving a note to share his plans.

Though Joel had been angry at the time, if they hadn't spent the next summer and autumn looking for Adam, neither Adam nor Joel would have found these women they now loved so deeply. Beaver Tail either, most likely.

So did that mean Adam had been wrong for leaving? The others would probably say God worked it all for His plan. Once upon a time, French might've believed them.

But if God had ever worked in his own life, the Almighty had left him the same day Colette had. The only difference was that Colette hadn't left of her own accord, she'd been forced to. If only he'd been old enough to leave home and travel along with her family. He'd been afraid to leave his mother alone though. Not with the way his father sometimes turned violent when the drink took over. Colette had promised to write, but he'd never heard once from her. There must not have been a way to send mail from Fort York.

Now, as he settled into his fur bedding, with a buffalo robe pulled over him against the cold spring night, he couldn't get the figure of that woman on horseback out of his mind. As a girl, Colette hadn't possessed that poise, not when they'd been running through the countryside, playing knights, or soldiers, or school teacher.

By the time she turned thirteen, her bearing had begun to change. That was about the time he'd kissed her, though he'd fallen in love with her long before then. Yet even the fourteen-year-old Colette who'd waved a tearful goodbye to him wasn't as poised and graceful—and tall—as the woman who'd ridden away from him today.

But that hair—the pale blonde. How likely was it another woman would have that same shade? It was a tad darker then her childhood color, but the same exact shade as her father.

What were the chances she would be riding through these wild mountains...in a United States territory, no less? So far from Fort York where her parents had moved her. Weeks maybe months away, depending on the season of travel.

But then, what were the chances any woman would be out here riding with five Piegan Blackfoot braves?

So many questions they made his chest ache, and not an

answer among them. Not if he kept laying here on this bed pallet, then rose in the morning and continued riding westward with his friends. He'd never get the answers.

If there was a chance, even a minuscule chance smaller than the mosquitoes that harassed them through the summer months, that woman was Colette... That the girl he'd spent a third of his life looking for, and had traveled the whole of Rupert's Land more than once to find... If she was lying somewhere in her own bed roll only a couple hours' ride away, how could he not go make certain? What if she were a prisoner?

The thought burned within him.

He could do what Adam had done, leave a note letting the others know where he was going. He'd find Colette—he could call her an old friend in his note, since the others wouldn't know her name. He'd tell them he'd be gone a week or two visiting with the friend and would catch up with them at Otskai's village. If they'd already left that place, he'd meet them at the town where Elan and Meksem hailed from.

Even if there was some kind of trouble that had driven Colette to this place, something he needed to take care of for her, that should give him enough time to do whatever necessary. He'd promised Colette he'd always love her. Always take care of her. They'd both promised. Though he'd only been thirteen at the time, he'd meant every word.

Maybe he could even bring Colette to meet these friends who had become like brothers, and even sisters, to him. After that, whatever Colette wanted, he would do. If she wanted to return to the Canadas, he would gladly take her there. Though his belly didn't hearken to the thought of living around so many people again. He'd much rather settle with her in these beautiful mountains. But wherever she was happiest, he would be happiest.

Easing down his fur covering, he scanned the other sleeping forms around him. He could just make out Beaver Tail's steady breathing, only because the man and his wife lay nearest French. Sneaking away without waking him would be a feat, as the man seemed to sleep with one eye open and both ears cocked.

If Beaver woke, French would just have to explain what he was doing. That would save him a note anyway. Beaver would likely let him leave without a stir. The man had uncanny insight. French could make him understand the importance of this without having to share details.

Sure enough, though French hadn't made any distinguishable noise that he knew of, as he finished rolling his furs in a bundle, Beaver Tail slipped out from the blanket he shared with Susanna.

The man watched as French looped his possibles bag over his neck and picked up his other packs. Beaver didn't awaken any of the others, only padded quietly behind French toward the horses.

When he reached Charlise, the mare he'd traded from the Nimiipuu, French turned to Beaver Tail and kept his voice low. "I think I recognized the white person who was with the Piegan Braves earlier today. He might be an old friend. I'm going to ride back and find out for sure. If it's who I think it is, I'll probably stay with them a few weeks, then catch up with you guys at one of the Nimiipuu towns. I'll look for you at Otskai's first, then go on to Elan's if need be."

At least he'd gotten the whole plan out before Beaver Tail responded. Though, the man thought first and spoke later.

Even now, it was six whole heartbeats before Beaver Tail finally parted his lips to speak. "A friend from before, when you were a boy?"

A knot of emotion clogged French's throat. How had the man guessed? That intuition at work.

He nodded. "Yes."

Beaver Tail didn't argue or beg him to stay, thank goodness.

He rose a hand to French's upper arm. It was the clasp of a brother, though Beaver Tail didn't usually show such emotion. "Go with God. And come back to us when you can."

The words seemed to say more than their simple meaning, but French didn't stop to read everything. He offered a returning grip to Beaver Tail's arm. "*Au revoir.*" The French farewell slid so easily from his tongue.

Then he released his friend, saddled his horse, and rode into the night.

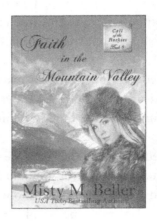

Get FAITH IN THE MOUNTAIN VALLEY at your Favorite Retailer!

ABOUT THE AUTHOR

Misty M. Beller is a *USA Today* bestselling author of romantic mountain stories, set on the 1800s frontier and woven with the truth of God's love.

She was raised on a farm in South Carolina, so her Southern roots run deep. Growing up, her family was close, and they continue to keep that priority today. Her husband and children now add another dimension to her life, keeping her both grounded and crazy.

God has placed a desire in Misty's heart to combine her love for Christian fiction and the simpler ranch life, writing historical novels that display God's abundant love through the twists and turns in the lives of her characters.

Connect with Misty at www.MistyMBeller.com

ALSO BY MISTY M. BELLER

The Mountain Series
The Lady and the Mountain Man
The Lady and the Mountain Doctor
The Lady and the Mountain Fire
The Lady and the Mountain Promise
The Lady and the Mountain Call
This Treacherous Journey
This Wilderness Journey
This Freedom Journey (novella)
This Courageous Journey
This Homeward Journey
This Daring Journey
This Healing Journey

Call of the Rockies
Freedom in the Mountain Wind
Hope in the Mountain River
Light in the Mountain Sky
Courage in the Mountain Wilderness
Faith in the Mountain Valley

Hearts of Montana
Hope's Highest Mountain
Love's Mountain Quest
Faith's Mountain Home

Texas Rancher Trilogy

The Rancher Takes a Cook

The Ranger Takes a Bride

The Rancher Takes a Cowgirl

Wyoming Mountain Tales

A Pony Express Romance

A Rocky Mountain Romance

A Sweetwater River Romance

A Mountain Christmas Romance

Made in the USA
Monee, IL
14 October 2023